Eduard Zeller

David Friedrich Strauss in his life and writings

Eduard Zeller

David Friedrich Strauss in his life and writings

ISBN/EAN: 9783742891402

Manufactured in Europe, USA, Canada, Australia, Japa

Cover: Foto ©Raphael Reischuk / pixelio.de

Manufactured and distributed by brebook publishing software
(www.brebook.com)

Eduard Zeller

David Friedrich Strauss in his life and writings

DAVID FRIEDRICH STRAUSS

IN

HIS LIFE AND WRITINGS

BY

EDUARD ZELLER

AUTHORISED TRANSLATION

WITH A PORTRAIT

LONDON
SMITH, ELDER, & CO., 15 WATERLOO PLACE
1874

PREFACE.

IMMEDIATELY AFTER the death of the man to whose memory the following pages are dedicated, I was requested by the Editor of the 'Swabian Mercury' to write a necrology on him for that journal. This I promised to do, only stipulating to be allowed a somewhat longer time, as other duties prevented me from undertaking it immediately. When, however, I proceeded to the execution of the task, during the last Easter vacation, I became speedily convinced that I could not keep my narrative, without incurring my own utter dissatisfaction with it, either in substance or extent, within the limits involved by its appearance in a daily journal. I therefore resolved to design it at once on a larger scale, and to comprise in it more than was compatible with its original object. The present memoir is the result.

It is not intended to present a biography, but a biographical delineation ; not a finished picture, but a preliminary sketch. In order to write the biography of such a man as Strauss, I should have required far more complete material and far more leisure than stood at my disposal at the present time. Moreover, the history of a life cannot be fully delineated until that life is so far removed from the present that the persons and the circumstances which influenced its course can be openly discussed on all sides without wounding the legitimate feelings and considerations of others. Even where no such scruples existed, distinct limits were imposed on my work by its whole plan and by the little time which I could bestow upon it. Much that I could have added I was obliged to withhold, because it would have too much disturbed the harmony of the whole. I have been obliged to pass over in silence, or with slight allusions, persons who stood in close connection with Strauss, and personal relations which he valued; for a narrative on a larger scale would alone have afforded sufficient scope to make the general reader acquainted with these persons and to render their relations intelligible to him. The principal figure moreover could not stand out with perfect distinctness if it were surrounded in its narrow framework by too many subordinate figures; who would likewise require to be treated with a certain amount of care in order to render them recognisable.

The basis of the following biography has been formed chiefly from my personal recollections, in addition to Strauss's works and a few published notices respecting him. These recollections extended over the greater part of Strauss's life; for I had known him even before he had left the University. Soon afterwards I had him as a teacher, and for several years I lived under the same roof with him; and from that period I kept up an intimacy with him which, from time to time, as our places of abode allowed of it, was revived by shorter or longer meetings. In addition to this, I have had the perusal of more than two hundred letters, extending from the end of the year 1835 to the last weeks of my friend's life. Where these sources have proved insufficient (which, however, was on the whole but rarely the case) I have gathered information from those who were in intercourse with him at different periods. A valuable completion to my own knowledge of him has, lastly, been afforded me by Strauss's own records of his life and by the poems which in the course of my work have been most kindly sent to me by his children.

From these aids I venture to hope that I have been sufficiently informed upon the subject I have undertaken, and that, much as this sketch is lacking in completeness, it is at any rate guarded from errors of any importance.

THE AUTHOR.

Berlin : *May* 1, 1874.

CONTENTS.

LIFE AND WRITINGS

OF

DAVID FRIEDRICH STRAUSS.

———•◦•———

CHAPTER I.

BOYHOOD.

THE Swabian race has at all times, and especially during the last century, been associated
with the intellectual life of the German people.
During this period it has produced a grand
succession of scholars and artists, of poets
and thinkers, whose name and influence have
far exceeded the limits of their narrow home,
and not unfrequently those of the German
language. But not many of these are to be
compared in endowments and historical importance with the man, the portrait of whose
life and character we shall sketch in the fol-

lowing pages. By his striking theological works, even as a young man, David Friedrich Strauss called forth a movement which not merely is still to be felt in this branch of science, but which had also a decided effect upon the philosophy and general culture of our own day. He subsequently enriched the history of literature, both in and out of Germany, with a considerable number of intellectual biographies, profoundly conceived and finely finished. In the second revision of his ' Life of Jesus,' fundamentally adhering to his earlier views, he brought to a final result the thirty years' labour of that German criticism on the Gospels to which he had himself given the impetus.

In his last work, which attracted such great attention, he not only combined his earlier critical labours into one artistic work insurpassable in its kind, but he also ventured, in express opposition to that which is regarded by most as unapproachable truth, to sketch the fundamental outline of a new theory of life more in harmony with the natural and historical knowledge of the present day, and with the present condition of thought ; and in so doing, at all events, whatever opinion we may hold as to the defensibility of his views, he raised questions, expressed ideas, and started problems, which will long furnish the profound investigator with a stimulant, and with matter for serious reflection.

But he did still more than this. He gave the world the living example of a man who, impelled by inextinguishable thirst for truth, never ceased to seek and to strive; whose development never paused, and was never lulled by the ease of possession and enjoyment; whom no authority deterred from examination and enquiry, and from candidly expressing without fear and secondary considerations whatever he discovered; who regarded it as the true vocation of his life to destroy prejudices, to prove the weakness of the shibboleths of time and parties, and to bring men from words to things, from indefinite ideas to distinct conceptions and certain observations; but at the same time of a man who valued mental culture still more than knowledge, and who, with the most extensive learning, and the widest interest in nature and humanity, sought above all for unity with himself, for the harmony and perfection of his inner life, and for the pure, undisturbed, and thorough development of his mental individuality.

This it was which caused not the least part of the attractive power and success of Strauss's writings. His readers felt that in him they had not to do merely with the scholar, the thinker, and the master in expression and language, but at the same time ever with the man himself. They found themselves, even in his strictly scientific works, and far more in his popular writings, brought face to face with a peculiar and richly cultivated being, and drawn into intimate communion with him; they felt themselves always excited and interested, always in excellent society; and this charm of personal intercourse with the clever and attractive author was with difficulty resisted by cultivated minds, even when they shrank from the two-edged critic, and crossed themselves in the presence of the heretic. Yet, for the same reason, his writings, however apparently, as objective works of art, they may have separated themselves from the person of their author, stand for ever in such close connection with him, that much in them cannot be fully understood and enjoyed unless to a certain extent we are acquainted with him.

Strauss was born on January 27, 1808, at Ludwigsburg, the same town in which his friends Justinus Kerner, Eduard Mörike, and Friedrich Vischer first saw the light; and to this his native city he clung with faithful attachment throughout his life. It afforded him moreover truly much that could fascinate the boy, and that could make the man look back to it from afar gratefully and longingly. It was not alone the paternal house and garden, the fresh air and the splendid playgrounds afforded by the broad streets and avenues of the secluded town and park, but he also enjoyed that comfortable limitation of burgher circumstances in which during the early years of life the development of mind and body thrives, as a rule, far better and more healthily than amid the noise and distractions of a capital. In addition to this, it possessed a school which, according to the requirements of the period, satisfied the demands for education up to

fourteen years of age. And as Ludwigsburg
was not only the principal garrison town of
the country, but also since its foundation had
been, with the adjacent Stuttgart, the residence
of its princes, it enjoyed so much connection
with public life, so much direct interest in the
traditions of Karl Alexander, who was said to
have wrung off the Devil's neck in the Ludwigsburg Palace, and of ' Herzog Karl,' of
Schubart and Schiller, and other personages
of more modern Würtemberg history, and
such a view of the movements which the
great period of the Napoleonic wars, and
subsequently the Würtemberg constitutional
struggles produced, that the boy's eye was not
likely to be too much occupied by petty and
narrow concerns.

The class to which Strauss belonged, and
in which he grew up, was, generally speaking,
that of the higher bourgeoisie, such as frequently existed at that period in a small south
German town, lying somewhat remote from
intercourse with the world. But while he
had inherited from his parents an individuality of a peculiar stamp, there was also in his
paternal home no lack of impressions and in-

fluences, which gave a peculiar turn to its development. His father was a retail merchant, whose outward position would have been good enough had he not, from unfavourable circumstances and his own mistakes, experienced losses which sensibly affected the comfort of the family and the tone of the house. With his fine talents and good education he would probably have fared better in some scholarly vocation than in an industrial one. Besides reading the more modern poets, he studied his Horace, Ovid, and Virgil in the original; and when he went into the country he delighted in sitting alone in the inn-garden with one of these classic authors in his hand. He had, as his son proudly states, an innate ability for written compositions of all kinds; he was moreover not without talent for poetry; he devoted more time to the cultivation of fruit and the rearing of bees than was good for his business, and in his leisure moments he was absorbed in the mysticism of Stilling's 'Grauen Mann.' In one word, he possessed a predominantly contemplative nature, inclined to intellectual interests; he was good-hearted, but his temper was irritable, quick,

and passionate ; and in the commercial deal-
ings of his retail trade, in which moreover he
took but little pleasure, he was not always so
courteous towards his customers as others of
his class were.

Strauss's mother was a distinguished wo-
man in her way, and he has himself depicted
her affectionately in a charming little sketch.[1]
Small and delicate in appearance, a simple,
homely, and contented nature, thoroughly
healthful in her judgment and feeling, cheerful, kindly, and full of good humour ; keenly
susceptible of all natural beauty, possessing a
ready appreciation for all that was naïve and
popular, and yet not excluded from higher intellectual interests ; in matters of religion just
as decidedly inclined to practical, comprehen-
sible, and rational views as her husband was to
belief in dogmas and mysticism.   A thorough
housewife, a loving,. judicious, and, when
necessary, even severe mother ; a faithful and
wise counsellor in difficulty to a husband not
very manageable at all times, she was the
good spirit of her home, and her grateful son
confesses that to her he owed the best that was

[1] Kl. Schr. N.F., 233 *et seq.*

in him. From her he not merely inherited the oval and finely-cut countenance which pleased and attracted at the first glance, with its nobly arched brow, and large, intelligent, and dark brilliant eyes ; in his mental physiognomy also we cannot fail to perceive the likeness to his mother. The clear mind, the delight in learning and the iron memory, which he points out in her, were not the only things in which he resembled her : fineness of feeling, free, cheerful humour, an apprecia-tion of all that was simple and natural, a capability of entering lovingly into the ima-gination of the people, of little children, and of the unlearned, a sensible apprehension of life, and the realistic bent of his nature, all this he had in common with her.

Nor was an admixture of the qualities of his father at the same time lacking. The impetuous temperament and the energetic will of his father had also been transmitted to him; the readiness in expressing him-self in writing, which he extols in his father, became in him a perfect art; the lite-rary and æsthetic inclinations of the one became in the other extensive study and a

fine understanding of literature, poetry, the
plastic arts, and even of music, for which he
originally possessed less natural genius. While
the father occasionally produced a successful
attempt at versification, the son has left us not
merely a collection of charming little poems, a
few specimens of which we shall presently mention, but he has never written anything, large
or small (as he himself remarks in one of his
notes), in which the poet within him was not
of use to him. While the one would have
been led by natural inclination to a career
of learning, the other found in science the
task of his life and his historical vocation.
Even the mystical tendencies of his father
were not, as we shall find, alien to him ; only
that to the one they presented a mere period
of transition, while to the other, less favoured
by natural endowments and by educational
advantages, they proved a permanent condition.

Strauss was the third child of his parents ;
the two elder ones, a girl and a boy, had died
before he was born. The latter he resembled
greatly both in character and appearance, and
even the name of the child, Fritz, devolved

upon him ; he himself, however, subsequently always signed his name in full, David Friedrich. Of his two younger brothers, only the one next him in age survived ; he was afterwards a manufacturer in Cologne, and died in 1863 from heart disease of long standing. An oration to his memory was written by his brother,[1] which warmly and eloquently delineates the solidity of his character, the freedom of his mind, his serious interest in the deepest subjects of enquiry, and the strength of his mind under his heavy suffering. Our Strauss, as his schoolfellow Vischer tells us,[2] was a somewhat weakly and delicately formed child, and was therefore excluded from the wilder play of his companions; and even at an early period, in quieter and more thoughtful amusements, his intellectual quickness and poetic imagination became apparent. At school, the same authority informs us, his vocation as a scholar betrayed itself in ready power of comprehension, in an excellent memory, and in conscientious

---

[1] Kl. Schr. N.F., 341 *et seq.*

[2] 'Krit. Gänge,' i. 84, in the sketch written in 1838, *Strauss and the Würtembergers;* a paper which has now acquired a fresh interest.

industry. It was therefore only an empty
boast when subsequently one of the teachers
of his boyhood, who lived to see the fame
of his pupil, claimed to himself the merit of
having laid the foundation of his future greatness by plentiful castigations.

In his fourteenth year, in the autumn of
1821, Strauss was placed in the lower Evangelical seminary at Blaubeuren, one of those
schools which were founded in Würtemberg
in the sixteenth century in former monasteries
for the education of future theologians, and
which therefore, even at the present day, are
still called monasteries. There are four of
these schools, and according to the regulation
of that period—a regulation recently altered—
the youths spent the four years intervening
until their admission to the University in the
same 'monastery' which they had entered at
fourteen. Living together in one building,
carefully superintended in their work and
behaviour, their education in the ordinary
branches of school learning is conducted by
the ephori of the seminary, two professors,
and two younger men, who, under the name
of *repetenten* (ushers), are entrusted with the

immediate supervision of the pupils. Strauss has himself given a lively description of the life and doings in the Blaubeuren seminary in his biography of Märklin. It was fortunate for him that this course of study and this establishment fell to his lot. Besides the beautiful situation of the little town in the Blauthal, lying on the southern declivity of the Swabian Alb, two miles from Ulm, the hospitable kindness of its inhabitants indemnified the scholars to a certain extent for absence from home and the restraint of the still somewhat monastic discipline ; but the main thing was, that among the fifty youths who were here passing together such a long and decisive portion of their life there were an unusual number of capable and even remarkably gifted minds, and of quick, witty, and assiduous characters ;[1] and that the most important branches of education were placed in the hands of two men such as the Professors Kern and Baur, who so happily supplied each other's deficiencies, and who, each in his own way, was so thoroughly equal to his vocation. Both of

[1] Cf. the names and characteristics given by Strauss himself in ' Märklin,' 21 *et seq.*

these subsequently, soon after Strauss's departure from Blaubeuren, joined the Faculty of Divinity at Tübingen, where he again had them as teachers, and from one of them, the famous founder of the ' Tübingen School,' he received the most lasting influence.   Classic literature and ancient history held the foremost place in the studies of the scholars, and into the spirit of these the ready mind of the pupil was initiated by his teacher ; and by means of them love for the ideal, desire for truth, and a taste for the beautiful and the great, were awakened and fostered within him.

CHAPTER II.

COLLEGE LIFE.

STRAUSS is among those in whom this seed-time produced the richest fruit. The four years at Blaubeuren were altogether of the utmost importance for the development of his mind. When he went there he was a shy boy, frightened at the noisy doings of his schoolfellows, and for the first few weeks he was a prey to home-sickness. When in the autumn of 1825, upon his admission into the Evangelical Theological College at Tübingen, he entered the University, he had ripened into a youth who, with all his merriment and amiability, unmistakably inspired both companions and teachers with respect; and though at first certainly, as Vischer says, no one would have foreseen the future critic in the proud overgrown youth, yet perhaps a deeper discerner of human nature would

have perceived the predisposition for such a
career in the severe scientific work, in the
independence of judgment, in the intellectual
originality, and in the decision of character,
which distinguished him even during his
student life.

According to the regulations at that time
existing with regard to the pupils of the
Evangelical College at Tübingen, two full
years were devoted to philosophical, philolo-
gical, and historical studies, and three more to
those of an exclusively theological character.
Strauss and his friends, however, had not here
the same good fortune in philosophy that they
had enjoyed at Blaubeuren. He himself tells
us in his ' Märklin ' (p. 31 *et seq.*) how much
they suffered from the dry character of the
instruction bestowed upon them. As regards
philosophy especially, the main subject of their
present studies, they found themselves here
predominantly thrown upon their own resources ; and it was then principally Schelling
who attracted Strauss, like most others, most
strongly, and inspired him with enthusiasm.
This bias was all the more natural, as at the
same time romantic poetry, the twin sister of

Schelling's natural philosophy, was exercising a magic influence over him. Repelled by the noise of ordinary student life, treating its illusions coldly and ironically, he had attached himself to a small circle of friends of poetic gifts and tastes, adherents of the romanticists, who raved with youthful enthusiasm for Novalis and Tieck, who ridiculed all that was low and common, and fabricated a wonderful mythology of their own, unknown and unintelligible to all others; whose labours, however, we must not too lightly estimate, since they have produced such charming results as 'Mörike's Poems.' With Mörike especially Strauss remained in close intimacy till his death; and he valued him no less as an amiable man overflowing with the wittiest humour, than as a poet whose songs bear comparison with few others in the whole range of German poetry, in purity of poetic tone, tenderness of feeling, and beauty of language. At that time he resigned himself entirely to the romanticist bias. He also successfully took part in the poetic attempts of his friends; and had not his other natural powers preponderated over his poetic gifts,

and prevented him from treating poetry
otherwise than as an ornamental adjunct of
his life, and induced him to use it in his literary labours only in combination with other
elements, he would undoubtedly have won an
esteemed name also as a poet.[1]

[1] I have already mentioned the poems which Strauss left
behind in manuscript. Some of those written during his
last illness will be subsequently inserted. In order, however,
to furnish an evidence from the earlier period of his life in
proof of the opinion just stated, I will here insert a song
which to my own mind may be compared in its melodious
simplicity with the most perfect productions of the kind
which we possess, whilst at the same time it affords us a
glimpse of Strauss' tender relations towards his father and
his paternal home, and of his delicate appreciation of nature.

THE LINDEN TREE.

Oh linden scent, oh linden tree !
Like childhood's dream ye come to me,
　　No dream without ye made.
Oh linden trees I love ye so ;
My father's house stood long ago
　　Beneath a lime tree's shade.

In summer when the lindens bloom,
How busily the bees will come
　　And seek the honied store.
My father took delight in bees ;
Hence, like a heritage these trees
　　Are sacred all the more.

The lime tree's shadow makes the wine,
And e'en a kiss too, doubly fine,
　　From childish lips when given.
Father, I bring this glass to thee ;
Thou lik'st not, 'neath the linden tree,
　　To sit with nought at even.

He was soon, however, led by his romanticist taste still further into mystic belief and
superstition, and this to a degree which we
should be perhaps inclined to doubt, had he
not himself informed us of the fact in his well-
known graceful delineation of Justinus Kerner.[1] He there tells us that at the beginning
of his University career he could not acquire
any taste at all for Kant, and could not understand his problems, but that, on the other
hand, he warmly embraced Schelling's intellectual opinions and also Jacobi's philosophy
of feeling ; that he soon ranked Jakob Böhme'
even above Schelling, and placed as firm a
belief in his sayings as he had hitherto done
in the Bible, revering in them, indeed, a more
deep and direct revelation than in the latter :
that with three friends he took a journey to a
fortune-teller, and on the way made the acquaintance of a shepherd who performed a
wonderful cure on one of the party ; that he
was absorbed in Kerner's history of two som-
nambulists, and that subsequently (it seems
to have been in the Easter vacation of 1827)
he visited the remarkable man himself at his

---

[1] 'Zwei friedliche Blätter.' Altona, 1839, p. 10, *et seq.*

charming residence at Weinsberg, and formed
a friendly intimacy not only with him, but
with his pleasing and agreeable wife, whom
Kerner subsequently made known to the
world as the ' Prophetess of Prevorst.'

We are inclined to enquire how it could be
that the mystic fanatic of that period should
become in a few years the cuttingly keen and
unmerciful critic which Strauss appears to us
in his ' Life of Jesus ' ?   Any one, however,
who is more closely acquainted with the history of the religious mind, knows that very
frequently mysticism both in individuals and
in ages has proved the transition from belief in
established authorities to the independent examination of transmitted tradition ; and those
who have more deeply penetrated into its
nature will perceive in this form of belief,
alien as it is to us, only one of the many
pupa-changes through which thought passes,
before its wings are sufficiently matured for
freer flights.

But in order to reach this independent
position, Strauss required a guide, and this he
found in the first place in Schleiermacher. To
his emancipating influence it was due that he

did not linger longer than was good for him
in the twilight of romantic dreamland, in
the vague depths of theosophy and amid
the alluring visions of somnambulism. And
Schleiermacher, especially at that time, was
better adapted than any other to render
him this service. As a philosopher, his pantheism aroused confidence in the disciple of
Schelling ; as a theologian, he met the religious
devotee and mystic with his Christian knowledge ; as an author, he attracted the romanticist by the æsthetic form of his discourses and
soliloquies ; whilst at the same time, with the
acuteness of his logic, he severed the threads,
one after another, which had hitherto bound
the mind of his disciple to unproved hypotheses and indistinct ideas. 'One bit of reflec-
tive matter after another,' says Strauss,
'found its way unobserved into our consciousness, and before we were aware of it, we
were standing on a wholly new mental soil,
from whence, looking back on the old fairy-
land of clairvoyance, magic, and sympathy,
everything appeared inverted.' In another
unpublished retrospect of his mental development, he remarks that it was only now on

first discovering in himself the gift of dialectic thought, that he was conscious of a genuine bias and true passion for study ; it was only from this period that he really learned, but that from henceforth he made the most rapid progress.

An evidence of this change of views, and a renunciation of his former belief in the wonders of somnambulism, appears in a criticism which Strauss wrote for the 'Hesperus' in 1830,[1] upon the various opinions on Kerner's 'Prophetess of Prevorst,' which had meanwhile appeared ; yet he still concedes more with respect to that belief than he would certainly have done subsequently. His friendly relation with Kerner was, however, only transiently disturbed by it ; and even afterwards, when Strauss directed his criticism against far more important articles of faith, the friendship of the two men was in no wise injured ;

[1] This paper is now published in his 'Characteristics and Critics,' p. 390 *et seq.* This criticism, and a discourse delivered by Strauss as a member of the Tübingen College, at the secular celebration of the anniversary of the Augsburg Confession on June 25, 1830, were the first things of Strauss that were published. The discourse is to be found in the description of the celebration published by the Tübingen Theological Faculty.

and as long as he lived at Heilbronn, he remained on terms of the closest and pleasantest intimacy with his marvel-loving neighbour at Weinsberg. Where such a belief appeared so simple, and combined with so many excellencies, as in Kerner, it was not difficult to Strauss to tolerate it; and, on the other hand, Kerner possessed such large and warm-hearted humanity, he was so entirely devoid of all the characteristics of a fanatic, though opposed to Strauss' views he was so sure of the soundness of his heart, and he himself, without knowing it, had such a strong sceptical vein within him, in the humour with which he regarded the world and trifled with it, that the sincerity and warmth of this friendship between the hyper-orthodox man and the supposed infidel cannot entirely surprise us. Strauss himself alluded to it in the above-mentioned article in the Hall Journals, and after Kerner's death in the funeral oration which was transferred from the ' Swabian Mercury' to the ' Kleine Schriften.'[1]

It was not, however, merely this one separation from Strauss' former circle of ideas

---

[1] N.F., 298 *et seq.*

which was involved in his breach with roman-
ticism, but when once this crisis in thought
had been reached, it necessarily affected all
the unproved dogmas and illogical hypotheses
that had accumulated in his mind. Strauss
and his friends were meanwhile promoted to
the study of theology. In this study, however, they were not thrown merely upon their
personal industry and upon books to the
same degree as in philosophy ; but the academical instruction afforded them in the one
far more advantages than in the other. When
Strauss had been a year at the University,
his Blaubeuren masters, Kern and Baur, had
been also removed there as professors of
Theology ; and if the merit of the former in
this branch of science was limited essentially
to clever grouping, to lucid and distinct representation, and to a just estimate of the
views of others, though his own lacked exactness and decision, with Baur a new spirit was
introduced into the theological faculty, a spirit
which was in time to repress the supernaturalism hitherto prevailing in it, and was to
place a new ' Tübingen School ' in the stead
of the old one ; namely, the spirit of historical

criticism. Schleiermacher's philosophy of
religion and dogmatic theology formed, however, also with Baur the more general
scientific substratum of this criticism ; and to
this later, after Strauss' university life was
over, was added the influence of Hegel's
system.[1]

Baur especially, among all Strauss' theological teachers, was the one who exercised a
deeper influence upon him. Of the three other
members of the faculty, he listened to Kern,
indeed, with advantage, but the weakness
and uncertainty of his theological views could
not long remain concealed from such a pupil
as Strauss. From Steudel, the senior of the
faculty, an excellent man, and personally most
estimable, he could not endure more than four
weeks of lectures ; and any one who knows
from personal experience the wearisome dis-
tortions of his supernaturalism, and the tor-
ture of his exaggerated style, or had heard
them depicted by Strauss,[2] would not blame
him for it. Schmidt, lastly, only attracted

---

[1] Cf. on this point my 'Vorträge und Abhandl.,' p. 381
et seq., 389 *et seq.*

[2] 'Märklin,' p. 38 *et seq.*

him at the end of his academical career
by directing his pulpit exercises.   It was
Schleiermacher, therefore, who exercised the
strongest influence upon Strauss also through
the medium of his teacher at the commence-
ment of his real theological studies ; and it is
a fact, not unimportant for the entire further
development of Protestant theology, that
he as well as Baur, the two founders, therefore, of the new tendency of theological
enquiry emanating from Swabia, passed
through the school of Schleiermacher before
they found their centre of gravity in that of
Hegel.

Whilst in North Germany the theological
systems of Schleiermacher and of Hegel are
wont to adhere to separate channels, strictly
severed from each other, here, from the first,
they flowed together in one current ; they
fertilised the soil and supplied mutual deficiencies.   From Schleiermacher, men learned
to understand religion in its peculiarity, and to
comprehend, to analyse, and to examine theological ideas in their historical distinctness :
in Hegel they were fascinated by the com-
prehensiveness of his views, by the strictness

of his dialectic development, and by the alluring prospect of comprehending all things in
their innermost principle, and of perceiving
in all that is and happens the one revelation
of the idea, fulfilling itself with dialectic necessity. Strauss could all the less resist the
attractive power of this system, as it was but
the logical continuation of that which he had
hitherto followed, namely, that of Schelling.
There was, indeed, at that time not much to
be learned respecting Hegel from the Tübingen lecturers ; but just as Strauss and his
friends had before sought out their own path
in philosophy, so they acted also now. It
was not till his last year at college that Strauss
read with Märklin and a few others Kant's
' Prolegomena,' which would now be looked
upon with other eyes than formerly ; and
afterwards Hegel's ' Phenomenology,' the very
work of this philosopher which was certainly
especially fitted to carry the reader from
Schelling to Hegel's later independent system, a transition which the author himself
passed through. The effect produced on him
by this work has been vividly depicted by
him in ' Märklin' (p. 54). On the other

hand, the young philosophers would not at
that time have relished Marheineke's dogmatics ; they were already too far advanced
in clearness of thought, and had studied their
Schleiermacher too thoroughly, to be able to
bear the scholastic formalism of this speculative orthodoxy, much as it is recommended
by Hegel himself, and profound as is the
wisdom which the North German Hegelians
perceive in it. The teaching of Baur, however, concurred with Schleiermacher's writings in disposing the Tübingen Hegelians to
assume a more critical demeanour with regard to transmitted theology than had been
usual in the school until Strauss made his
eventful appearance. For little as this theologian at that time had attained to the just
freedom of criticism and the just expansion
of historical views which distinguished him
later,[1] the lectures which Strauss heard him
deliver upon Church history, the history of
doctrinal theology, symbolism, the Acts of
the Apostles, and the Epistles to the Corin-
thians, exhibited not merely, as may be supposed, much scholarly learning, but were also

---

[1] Cf. Strauss' ' Märklin,' p. 39 *et seq.* ; p. 51.

replete with exciting ideas calculated to arouse mental freedom;[1] and although the teacher was not at that time perfectly settled in his own views, he was able perhaps all the more to give those apt scholars who were long familiar with him an insight into the mental work of a great and genuinely scientific character.

In the autumn of 1830 Strauss concluded his theological studies with a brilliant examination. At the same time he obtained two academical prizes for preaching and catechising. He was next obliged to exercise himself in the practical service of the Church, and for this purpose, in accordance with the Würtemberg system, he was appointed deputy (*vikar*) to a country clergyman, Pastor Zahn, at Kleiningersheim, a man in feeble health though still young. Owing to the smallness of the parish the business of this office was not so considerable as not to leave him sufficient leisure for the eager continuation of his theological and philosophical

[1] See further remarks on the subject in my 'Vorträge und Abhandl.,' p. 412 *et seq.*

studies. His new abode, picturesquely situated on a height above the Neckar, possessed, in addition to its fresh air, beautiful prospect, and pleasant intercourse with numerous neighbours, the further advantage that it was scarcely more than four miles from Ludwigsburg, and allowed of constant visits to the paternal home. The relation between mother and son, as the latter ripened in years, here became more and more intimate. He was her pride and her consolation, and the confidant of the cares which for many years had burdened her heavily. Moreover, the turn which his theological convictions had recently taken could not possibly be displeasing to the practical and intelligent spirit in which she conceived religion. It was otherwise in this respect with the father ; yet this circumstance seems at that time to have caused no disturbance between the two, widely sundered as their opinions must even then have been.

In his village parish Strauss was very popular as a preacher ; and subsequently, when under-master (*repetent*) at Tübingen, he was liked by the lower orders no less than by the more highly cultivated. His discourses, with all the intrinsic value of their contents, were distinguished also by an exemplary popularity. He never introduced speculations and criticism where they were unsuitable. He adhered to the practically religious tenor of the Bible precepts and narratives, and he treated these in the simplest manner, with distinctness and life, while the effect produced on his hearers was assisted by a clear and pleasing voice. The same may be said of his catechising, and in this, besides his dialectic readiness and his logical digestion of the ideas he had acquired, the facility with which he was able to transport himself into the minds of children, and to follow out their answers, was also of service to him. Nevertheless he spent only three quarters of a year in his office of deputy, for in the summer of 1831 he received the order to undertake the duties of a professor who had recently died at the college of Maulbronn. He had here to give instruction in Latin, history, and Hebrew to about thirty youths

on the point of passing to the University ;
and this task also, unexpectedly as it had
devolved upon him, he discharged so well
that he gained the most undivided love and
esteem of his pupils, among whom was the
author of this sketch of his life.

CHAPTER III.

THE LIFE OF JESUS.

In October 1831, Strauss went to Berlin, in order to become personally acquainted with the men to whom he felt he owed the most as regarded his scientific life, and to enjoy their instruction; and in so doing, above all others, not even excepting Schleiermacher, he had Hegel in view. Scarcely, however, had he introduced himself to the great philosopher and attended his first lectures, than, on November 14, Hegel was suddenly carried off by cholera. Strauss heard of this event, which so sadly crossed his plans, from Schleiermacher, when he was paying him his first visit, and startled by it, he exclaimed, to the evident displeasure of his host, 'It was for his sake that I came here!'

For a moment he now thought of leaving Berlin again, but he thought better of it, and

had no occasion to repent of his decision.
The capital of the Prussian state and the first
of the German universities, which Berlin indisputably was, afforded him such rich material
for culture, that we must attach essential value
to the winter which he spent there in the
maturing of his mind and the enlargement of
his knowledge.   He found himself in a new
world; he made the most eager use of the help
which it afforded him, and he formed many
valuable personal friendships.   He associated
with Hegel's widow, with Marheineke, Hitzig,
Gans, and other members of the Hegelian
school ; most closely of all he attached himself to Vatke, with whom for a long time
he planned the joint editorship of a periodical.
He was moreover a close attendant at Schleiermacher's sermons and lectures ; and though
in the latter the ' quicksilverlike volubility ' of
the dialectics was repugnant to him,[1] he owed
to them nevertheless many a suggestion ; and
the work which first made his name famous
and feared, received its impetus from Schleiermacher's lecture on the Life of Jesus, which

---

[1] Cf. the interesting remarks upon Schleiermacher's lecture
in the treatise which we shall presently mention : ' Der
Christus des Glaubens,' p. 5 *et seq.*

he knew from the transcripts of it made by its hearers, and which at any rate acted as a suggestion from the opposition it aroused in him.

Even at Tübingen, as he himself tells us,[1] it had appeared to him that the point in Hegel's system of most importance to theology was the distinction between active representation (*Vorstellung*) and pure theory (*Begriff*), and soon the main question for him became this, What is the bearing of the above-named distinction on the historical portion of the Bible, especially of the Gospels; are these included in the theoretic content of religion, or do they only form a part of its representative media, with which the fundamental religious conceptions are not indissolubly incorporated? He himself was inclined to decide in favour of the second of these assumptions; and he conceived the idea of a dogmatic theology which, from this point of view, was not merely to trace back the growth of ecclesiastical dogmas to biblical bases, but was also to carry out their solution by deism and rationalism, in order at length to establish them

---

[1] ' Streitschriften,' part 3, p. 57 *et seq.*

again theoretically in a purified form.   He
resolved, however, to limit himself first of all
to the more special task of completing the
'Life of Jesus,' which, according to his first
plan, sketched during his residence in Berlin,
was to have been designed in a similar manner to his proposed work on dogmatic theology.   It was to present in three parts, first
the Life of Christ according to the Gospels,
the Life of Christ in believers, and the reconciliation of the two in the second article of
the apostolic symbolum.   This was to be
followed by a critical section analysing the
Life of Christ historically.   In the third section, however, all that had been annulled
was to be dogmatically re-established.   For
this work Strauss intended to make use of
Schleiermacher's before-mentioned lectures ;
and if he found himself repelled by them, according to his own statement, at almost every
point, he nevertheless, he does not neglect
to add, ever owed to this repulsion the closer
fixing of his attention to many questions.
That he could never form any personal intimacy with Schleiermacher was to be antici-
pated after their first meeting.   This was the

case also subsequently with others of his
countrymen, who, as Hegelians, met with an
extremely cool reception with him, however
warm may have been their own feelings of
respect for the great theologian, and however
sincere their desire to learn from him.[1]

After half a year's residence at Berlin,
Strauss returned home, and soon after the
beginning of the summer term he was appointed under-master (*repetent*) at Tübingen,
where he renewed in the most agreeable and
useful manner his former social and scientific
intercourse with those of his university friends
who were already installed in the same capa-
city in the Evangelical College, or were installed soon after him.   By the students, and
especially by his former Maulbronn pupils,
his arrival was longingly looked for, as his
lectures promised more vigorous and palat-
able food for the mind than they had been
accustomed to meet with from the other
teachers of philosophy.   Nor were they
deceived in their expectations.   Strauss
began at once a course upon logics and metaphysics, which was followed in the succeeding

[1] Strauss' ' Märklin,' p. 78 *et seq.*

winter by the history of philosophy since
Kant, and the explanation of Plato's Feast,
and in the summer of 1833 by the history of
morals.   These lectures had a brilliant success; and still more than the number of
hearers they attracted, was the enthusiastic
impression they produced.   They acted
like a beneficent rain upon barren ground;
that deeper philosophical interest, which
hitherto had been so little cared for at
Tübingen, now for the first time met with
open acknowledgment and abundant satisfaction in a lecture room; and as Strauss now
decidedly took his stand upon Hegel's philosophy, this system became increasingly disseminated by his lectures; and whilst it had
hitherto been only the private possession of a
few select minds, it now became common
property.   Hegel could not, indeed, have
desired a better interpreter than he here
found.   The clearness of explanation and
the spirited vigour of expression rendered
even such a difficult subject as Hegel's Logic
intelligible to the understanding; and Strauss,
at that stage of his opinions, found no cause
for any thorough alterations in it, or for criti-

cising its whole procedure. With greater scientific independence he regarded his material in his lectures on the ' History of Philosophy,' and the excellences of his style of treatment had here an equally rich opportunity of rendering themselves apparent. His discourse adhered for the most part to the carefully prepared written form. Strauss himself subsequently expresses his opinion in his 'Memoir of Spittler'[1] that this scholar could have been no Swabian if free delivery had presented no difficulty to him. But at the same time he was so animated and interesting, that his listeners were constantly struck by the externals of his style, and their attention to the subject was kept up ; and among the many who at that time listened to Strauss, so far as they are yet among the living, there is not one who does not remember with thankfulness and pleasure the hours in which he followed his words.

Nevertheless Strauss' academical labours were only of short duration. Throughout them he had never lost sight of his plan of writing a Life of Jesus, and in order to find the

[1] 'Kl. Schr.,' i. 77.

necessary time for this, he relinquished his
lectures in the autumn of 1833, after three
terms.   The longer the task which he now
undertook had occupied him previous to its
execution, the more rapid was its present progress.   A rare power of work was combined
in him with an equally great delight in work ;
to brilliant talent was added thorough scientific
culture; and acute and well-disciplined thought
was united with a perfect command of language and expression, so completely inherent
in him by nature, that he himself remarks in
his note-book, that he was never in the least
conscious of wrestling with language, or, indeed, of any special effort ; that in everything
which he wished to express, the right word
always occurred of itself, and that unsought
for ; the suitable form and appropriate tone
presented itself for every kind of subject.
The impulse with which the work originated
was so strong in the author's mind, that a
year after the beginning of its first preparatory
arrangement, the whole, with the exception
of the concluding dissertation, in all more
than fourteen hundred printed pages, was
ready in manuscript.   The first volume ap-

peared in the summer, the second in the
autumn of 1835, under the title, 'The Life of
Jesus Critically Considered.' Thus the die
was cast, the step was ventured, which was to
decide Strauss' scientific importance, his position in his age, and the future course of his
life.

The 'Life of Jesus,' as he had formerly
designed it, had now become a criticism of the
evangelical accounts of the Life of Christ;
and although this criticism was followed by a
concluding dissertation, which promised to
exhibit the dogmatic value as unimpaired,
still this did not merely amount to only a few
pages in extent, but it led, as we shall see, to
no result which could change the critical
character of the work. The criticism moreover, and this has been urged against it, and
also really denotes the point at which it required completion, was not a criticism of the
Gospels, but of the *Gospel story*; in other
words, it was limited in its essential purpose
to the question whether, and how far, all that
is told us by our four Gospels really happened.
The preliminary question on the other hand,
how it stood with these writings themselves

as such—where, when, and by whom, under
what circumstances and with what intention,
they were composed,—was not taken further
into consideration than in the brief authentication [1] that none of our Gospels can be
proved as the work of a man, the period
and circumstances of whose life would render
impossible the assumption of incorrectness
of statement; that consequently criticism
was perfectly free to expunge from their
narratives everything which carried with it
the appearance of being untrue to history.
These appearances were to be found in various
statements, in their contradiction with the
facts of the case as attested by other accounts,
and more frequently and in more important
instances in the contradiction existing between
the different Gospel statements themselves.
The most decided indications of non-historical
truth were, however, in Strauss' eyes the
miracles, which are scattered so freely throughout the Gospel narratives, that scarcely any
incident is recorded in them which is not
intermixed more or less superficially with
miracles. On this point he had, however,

---

[1] I., 62 *et seq.* 1st edition.

to deal with two classes of interpreters into which, at the time he wrote his book, theologians were almost without exception divided, namely, the supernaturalists, who adhered to the actual occurrence of the miracles, and the rationalists, who acknowledged the miracles, it is true, as such, but endeavoured all the more to rescue the truth of the Biblical narratives by a natural explanation of the miraculous incidents which they recorded. Strauss, for his part, was satisfied with neither of these. If the exegesis of the ancient Church emanated from the double hypothesis that the Gospels contained in the first place history, and in the second place a record of the supernatural, and if rationalism rejected the second of these hypotheses, in order to cling only all the more firmly to the first, it is impossible, as he says (I. v.), for science to halt in this manner midway ; all other considerations must be set aside, and it must first be proved whether, and how far, we stand at all on an historical basis in the Gospels. This principle he followed out with the utmost severity and exactness through the whole of our Gospels, from beginning to end. He analysed their narra-

tives, he studied their different views and
explanations, he examined how they agreed,
on the one side, with the demonstrable opinion
of the narrator, and on the other with the
general laws of the event ; and in this way he
arrived at length at the result, that a great
part, indeed, as regards its extent, the greater
part of the Gospel records contained either
no historical matter at all, or historical matter
so disfigured that it was scarcely recognisable
as such.   And in this he did not limit himself
to those points which in themselves have no
longer any deeper significance to the Christianity of our own day, and which are adhered
to by most persons more for the sake of the
principle of derogating in nothing from Scrip-
tural authority, such as the visible ascent into
heaven, the history of the birth and childhood,
and various miracles ; but also the words of the
Christ of St. John almost entirely, and even
a narrative as deeply affecting dogmatic theology as that of the resurrection.   In short,
everything that would oblige us to see more
than a man in the founder of Christianity, or
to raise him above the conditions of his age
and his surroundings, was set aside by him as

non-historical.   If, however, these narratives,
and these distinct parts of the narratives, are
not historical, what are they then, and how
are we to explain their origin ?   Certainly
not, answers the critic, by historical recollec-
tion ; equally little by free, conscious inven-
tion ; but by an unconscious, unintentional
fiction, which, as such, cannot be the work of
one man, but only of a body of men, of the
community in whose bosom these narratives
have been formed.   Those non-historical
narratives are, therefore, in a word, legends
which our Evangelists found existing in the
Christian community of their age, and which
they received from oral tradition, fully believing in their truth.   The formation of these
legends was not, however, on the whole, left
to chance ; little as they proceeded from conscious calculation, their authors were uncon-
sciously guided by certain ideas and interests
disseminated in the earliest Christian communities ; they are not simple legends, but
legends originating from a dogmatic tendency
—they are *myths.*

To the former interpretations of the Gospel history, Strauss opposed a mythical inter-

pretation. There was, he thinks, a double
interest at work in the formation of the legends
respecting Christ; the founder of Christianity
was on the one side to be glorified as much
as possible, and on the other side the fulfil-
ment of the Messianic prophecy was to be
proved in Him ; He was to be represented as
the one in whose person, acts, and fate all
those characteristics were combined which,
proceeding partly from Old Testament prophecy, and partly from later interpretations
and amplifications, belonged to the idea of the
Jewish Messiah of that period. In accordance
with these views, he estimated the substance
of the Gospel tradition, and so far as the
critic could not regard it as historical, he endeavoured to explain it as mythical. This non-
historical portion is, indeed, as we have already
remarked, very great ; and nothing is left as
the historical balance of criticism—and this
Strauss did not attempt to gather together
expressly, and to digest historically, in the
work under consideration—but the general
outline of the Life of Jesus, from his public
appearance to his death on the cross.

Nevertheless, not merely in the preface to

his first volume, but also in the concluding
dissertation of his second volume, Strauss
adhered to the statement that the critic of the
19th century, differing from the free-thinker
and the naturalist, is conscious of the substance
of the Christian religion as identical with the
highest philosophical truth ; and after having
in the course of his criticism only exhibited
the distinction of his conviction from belief in
Christian history, he promises to establish it
also on the ground of identity. If, however, we
indeed look more closely into the matter, we
perceive that dogmatic criticism had already
carried him much further than was consistent with Hegel's propositions with regard
to the relation between pure theory (*Begriff*)
and active representation (*Vorstellung*),
however evidently these pervade the above
remarks. Pursuing the history of doctrinal
theology, he follows the formation of ecclesiastical Christology and the attacks to which
it has been subjected, and thoroughly accepts
the results of the criticism which Schleiermacher and rationalism had suffered pa-
tiently ; on the other side he blames rationalism for having stinted the belief of the

Church in order to maintain itself in unison
with it; he points out, however, also to
Schleiermacher, that the ideal and the historical in his Christ in nowise actually coin-
cide, as he desired they should ; that knowledge as well as belief falls short with him ;
and he can just as little convince himself of
the defensibility of attempts to deduce from
Hegel's propositions of the unity of the divine
and human nature a God-man as an historical
personality.   The idea, he declares, is not
wont to disburden all its fulness in one person and to be parsimonious with all others,
but it loves to diffuse its riches in a
variety of individuals who mutually supply
what is lacking in the other.   This is the
key, he states, of all Christology, that an idea,
instead of an individual, is placed as the subject of the predicates which the Church at-
tributes to Christ. Conceived in an individual,
a God-man, these predicates are contradictory;
in the idea of the race they harmonize.
Humanity alone is the Incarnate God ; of it
alone can all that be stated (as he carries out
in detail), which we can attribute to no single

man without falling from one contradiction into another.

That serious difficulties may, indeed, arise to the practical theologian in his relation to his congregation in this transition from active representation to pure theory, even though he may be able to set his own mind at rest on the point, Strauss does not attempt to dispute. But this collision, he remarks, is not caused by the inconsiderate curiosity of a single individual, but is necessarily brought about by the course of time and the advance of Christian theology; and while many guard against it by abstaining from study and thought, or even from freedom of speech and writing, there are others who, in spite of all opposition, freely confess what can no longer remain concealed. 'And time will show,' he adds, in conclusion, 'which of the two is of greater service to the Church, to humanity, and to truth.'

E

CHAPTER IV.

THE DIE CAST.

THE 'Life of Jesus,' immediately on its appearance, produced a sensation rarely made
by a theological or philosophical work.   If it
was not for the first time that mythical elements in the Bible had been spoken of, this
assumption had been hitherto far more timidly
advanced, and in the New Testament especially it had been limited to a few narratives,
and those of less importance in a dogmatic
respect.   Now, on the contrary, it was applied
to the whole of the Gospel tradition to such
an extent, and with such regardless logical
consistency, that it threatened utterly to explain away the historical substance, or to
shrivel it to the smallest compass.   And this
result was not an assertion lightly thrown out,
but it was obtained by an investigation entering with scholarly profoundness into every

detail, and by a comprehensive examination
of different opinions, discussing every proba-
bility, and closing every way of escape to its
adversaries. Men had not to deal with the
coup de main of a bold partisan, but with a
well considered stroke, aimed with masterly
dialectic power, with the force of an attack directed against the central point of their own
position and carried out with profound scientific conviction. And this attack appeared all
the more dangerous as the work in which it
was made was also distinguished by a beauty
of language and a readiness and clearness of
expression, such as had been hitherto almost
unprecedented in scientific works in Germany.
Can we wonder if, immediately after the appearance of the work, the most violent storm
burst forth against the presumptuous critic;
if those called upon, and those not called upon,
hastened to extinguish the dangerous fire-
brand; if he was attacked by a general levy
of the people in addition to well-disciplined
troops and was fought with unpermitted and
worn-out weapons, in addition to those more
pertinent in character and more in harmony
with scientific customs? For several years

not merely in Germany almost all theological literature hinged upon Strauss's 'Life of Jesus,' but other lands also took a lively interest in it, as its English and French translations testify. Hundreds of refutations, of every tone and size, appeared ; as early as 1838 the third edition of the work had become necessary, and this was soon after followed by a fourth ; and those who can speak of the period from personal remembrance, and who have had opportunity of perceiving the tone of feeling in various parts of Germany, must confess that no scientific or literary production has ever since occasioned such general and lively excitement in the minds of men.

What sort of a man, however, was it against whom all these attacks were directed, and who had thrown down this apple of discord to the age ? The question suggested itself all the more readily as the author of the 'Life of Jesus' had hitherto only introduced himself to to the notice of the scientific world by a few reviews, in which, it is true, unusual critical and literary ability was already to be perceived. But, as is often the case, those who judged of him only by his writings and their immediate effects conceived almost infallibly an erroneous idea of him ; and this even when they did not belong to the great number of those who did not and would not understand that others besides immoral and reprobate men may oppose the religious notions to which they themselves cling, and that a man may be compelled by his conscience and his love of truth to doubt and dispute that which is most sacred and unapproachable.

Even in his outward appearance Strauss but little corresponded with the idea which probably most people formed of him from his works ; and few would have divined the bold writer pitilessly analysing his subject with scientific coldness in the delicate lines of the youthful countenance, the slight bend of the head, and the contemplative down-cast eye, which with its peculiar action, indicating weakness of the organ, gave an impression of almost girlish shyness.   •

To those who knew him personally he appeared an intelligent, highly cultivated man, and in more intimate circles he was a

lively, cheerful, and agreeable companion and
an excellent narrator, possessing the keenest
appreciation of all that was naïve and humor-
ous, both in a kindly and comic point of view ;
at the same time, however, he had a tender, fine-feeling, and artistic nature, which
in its purity and inward reserve shunned
all disturbance, to which any personal pre-
eminence cost a certain self-command, and
which in any rude collision was easily wounded
and drew back shyly within itself.   With all
this there were sharply stamped those traits
of a manly character which struck the eye at
once on the author's public appearance :
quickly and powerfully excited anger, a
decided and energetic will, and a scientific
courage, which, if necessary, would defy the
opinion of the whole world.   It was not,
however, very easy to find the inner point of
unity in qualities apparently so widely differing : to perceive in depth of feeling the
birthplace of the energetic will, in delicacy of
æsthetic taste one of the roots of that critical
sagacity, in the natural delight in whatever
was genuine and naïve that feature of his
mind which made Strauss in science also a

foe to all misty ideas and all abstract for-
mulas, to all that was artificial and inwardly
untrue ; to trace back to the same source
the sensitiveness to disturbance, of whatever
kind it might be, and that scientific courage
connected with it : namely, to that idealism
which in the first place desired to mould into
harmony his own inner life and to bring it to
a satisfactory conclusion, but which for that
very reason turned vigorously and regardlessly against aught that demanded an
acknowledgment from him which he felt compelled to refuse.

How much Strauss had ventured with,
his work he was soon to prove. Even before the appearance of his second volume he
was removed from his post at Tübingen, and
in its place he was assigned a position as
teacher in the lyceum of his native town. It
would indeed have been best to have declined
this office from the first, and to have come
forward as teacher of philosophy at Tübingen,
where his admission into the philosophical
faculty would scarcely have been opposed,
and perhaps even his appointment would not
at that time have met with that opposi-

tion which subsequently certainly excluded
all who shared Strauss's views from obtaining
even a philosophical professorship. But
whether it was that his old bourgeois respect-
ability shrunk from such an uncertain career,
or that he was unwilling to fetter himself to a
philosophical course of instruction whilst he
felt himself a master in theological criticism,
and that he here saw so much work still before him, Strauss consented to the unwel-
come office, and after remaining a few months
at Tübingen outside the college, he entered
upon his duties in the autumn of 1835.

Residence, however, in a town which
afforded him neither scientific resources nor
scientific intercourse, could scarcely permanently suit him, and the instruction of im-
mature boys, which he had to impart for
seventeen hours weekly, could not possibly
be pleasing to him. To this other things
were moreover added. He resided at Ludwigsburg, and, as was natural and under
existing circumstances totally unavoidable, in
his parents' house; but by this means he
came into constant dispute with his father,
who had from the beginning disapproved of

his opinions and their bold expression in the
' Life of Jesus,' and was all the more angry
with his degenerated son the more violent
grew the storm which the latter had called
forth against himself. There were painful
scenes : Strauss's mother had much to suffer
under the incongruity existing between husband and son, and it was full time for the
latter to withdraw from a position that had
become intolerable, when in the autumn of
1836 he resigned the post which he had
occupied for a year, and proceeded to Stuttgart, in order to devote his time uninter-
ruptedly to his literary pursuits.[1]

The inducement to take this step was not
wanting. Even in the first year after the
completion of the ' Life of Jesus ' a second
edition became necessary, and this speedily,
as we have already said, was followed by a
third and fourth. Strauss used this opportunity for renewed examination, correction, and
completion of his work in the most conscientious manner, nor did he exclude himself
from the objections of his adversaries ; but

---

[1] Strauss alludes to the state of things referred to in his
' Kl. Schr.,' *N. F.*, p. 264 et seq.

after having made considerable concessions
to them in the third edition, especially as
regards the Gospel of St. John, he became
finally convinced that he had ceded to them
more than was necessary and than was consistent with the logical carrying out of his
views, and in the fourth edition he drew back
again most of these concessions. In addition
to the revision he was, however, also occupied
in the defence of his work. After all the
attacks and reproaches, the objections, mis-
understandings, and misconstructions, to
which his work and himself had been ex-
posed since the first appearance of the ' Life
of Jesus,' it seemed to him the fitting time to
come to a thorough explanation and to settle
matters distinctly with the most distinguished
of his adversaries, as he could do this by
adding occasional notes to the second edition ;
and in so doing he in no wise thought
alone of warding off attacks, but he acted
also on his side on the offensive : he desired not merely to examine the defensibility
of the arguments which had been raised
against him, but also to delineate the views
and procedure of his adversaries, to bring

their weakness to light, and by a comprehensive analysis of his scientific and literary
character to decide the question as to his
right to come forward.

In this spirit he discussed in the first of
the three parts of his ‘ Polemical Papers ’[1]
‘ Dr. Steudel on the Self-delusions of the
Wise Supernaturalism of the present Day ; ’
in the second, he considered the attacks of
two laymen, Eschenmayer and Menzel, one
of whom had taken part in the theological dispute in as fanatical a spirit, and the other in
as overbearing a manner, as they were both
ignorant and uncalled for ; the third was devoted to Hengstenberg and the Evangelical
Church Journal, to the Hegelian school and
the journals for scientific criticism, and to the
medium theology and its main organ, ‘ Studies
and Critics.’ In these discussions also the
same masterly power was displayed as in the
‘ Life of Jesus.’ Strauss’s ‘ Polemical Papers ’
are a controversial work, and no more brilliant production of the kind has ever appeared

---

[1] ‘ Streitschriften zur Vertheidigung meiner Schrift über
das Leben Jesu und zur Characteristik der gegenwärtigen
Theologie,’ part 3, 1837.

in German literature since the time of Lessing. Whether he was demonstrating to Steudel the self-delusions of a supernaturalism which was infected with rationalism far more deeply than he was aware of, or pointing out the mistakes of his apology, and the distortion of his interpretation, or proving to Eschenmayer, the spiritualist philosopher, the dim unreasonableness of his fanaticism ; whether he was bringing forward Menzel as a literary historian and critic, or Hengstenberg as an inquisitor ; whether he was discussing with the Hegelian school the theological consequences of its system, or with Ullmann the extent of the concessions which this theologian had made to criticism ; everywhere we find the accurate and thorough work, the certain knowledge, and the victorious dialectic power which had already distinguished the earlier production ; and at the same time a'readiness of expression, a profusion of startling allusions, of distinct and striking points, a keenly appropriate · characterisation of persons and views, and a well-considered and not unfrequently annihilating humour, which could here be brought to bear far more strongly than before.

As regards subject, the explanations with the Hegelians and with Wolfgang Menzel possess the greatest interest ; the former, because not only did the scholastic divinity of the old Hegelian orthodoxy, the championship of which had been assumed in this instance by Bruno Bauer, receive its due rebuff, but Hegel's own position with regard to the questions of Gospel criticism and Christology was thoroughly investigated ; the latter because it combined with the chastisement of an assuming and superficial writer, who for ten years had taken the lead in criticism and in literary and political history, and had maintained a perfect terrorism with his moral political inquisition, an abundance of sound opinions and acute observations, some with respect to different men, such as Goethe and Johannes Müller, and some upon more general questions, such as the applicability of the moral standard to art. Strauss's intended continuation of the ' Polemical Papers ' was not arrived at, as he was interrupted in their preparation by the necessity of a third edition of the ' Life of Jesus,' and that which was to have occupied his attention in the former was in all essential points introduced into the main work itself.

In December 1837 Strauss wrote to me just as the third edition of the 'Life of Jesus' was passing through the press, and declared that when once he had finished his task he would not very soon again use his theological pen. And it is true that during this and the two following years we have several works by him which stand in no connection with his theological critical investigations, such as the notices of Hoffmeister's and Hinrich's works on Schiller, of Auerbach's Spinoza, of some writings on magnetism and spiritual possession, two papers on which (by Kerner) he had reviewed in 1836, and other things; also the before-mentioned account of Kerner; and lastly the valuable treatise upon Schleiermacher and Daub, entering fully into the characters, writings, and opinions of the two men. If the latter belongs, in its main purport at any rate, to the history of theology, another production of the same period, the 'Discourses upon the Transitory and the Permanent in Christianity,' affords a still more direct proof of the fact

that at that time Strauss was on the fair way
to lay aside his theological pen. These discourses are nothing else than an answer to
the question as to what was still lacking to
views of religion and Christianity such as his ;
and this answer is given in such a conciliatory spirit that its author was justified when
he published them in 1839 with the article
upon Kerner, under the title of ' Zwei friedliche Blätter' ('Two Peaceful Papers'), whilst
in the same year he joined his treatise upon
Schleiermacher and Daub with his other
smaller works, in the ' Characteristics and
Critics.' Here, it is true, the main results of
his critical work were partly repeated and
partly expanded in their dogmatic aspect.
He explains shortly and concisely how the
prospect of future recompense cannot, and
ought not, to have the significance of a moral
incitement ; how equally little the resurrection
of Christ could affect the ground of our belief
in Him, even if its actual occurrence and its
wonderful character were more surely established than is in truth the case ; how the
redemption by his vicarious sufferings and
death is no longer consistent with our moral

notions, and therefore his death as an external fact is of value not so much as regards
religion itself, but rather as regards the history of religion and metaphorical expression ;
how only those of the miracles of the Gospel
story are to be accepted as probable which
may be considered, it is true, as somewhat
unusual, but not as somewhat supernatural,
and which therefore possess no demonstra-
tive power of a religiously dogmatic nature ;
how neither the supernatural origin nor the
theandric nature of Christ finds a place in
our conception, and the worship of genius is
the only thing which is left to the cultivated
minds of the present time. But this very
thought, following out still further the sug-
gestions which he had already thrown out on
the subject in the third part of the ' Polemical
Papers,' serves him now as a bridge for obtaining for the founder of Christianity the
prerogative of being the highest of his kind.
This prerogative is more accurately established by the fact that the religious genius.
is, as such, distinguished from all others, and
is exalted above them by the harmonious
perfection of the inner life ; in the sphere of

religion itself, however, the highest, the perfect unity of human self-consciousness with
divine consciousness, is only attained when,
as in Jesus, the man is decided in every
action entirely by this alone, and at the same
time knows and feels this decision as his own
self-determination.

Strauss here, therefore, so far approxi-
mates to Schleiermacher's Christology that
he declares that just as little as mankind will
ever be without religion, so little will they
ever be without Christ, and the less we scru-
pulously adhere to dogmas and opinions
which must tend to impede thought, the more
surely does Christ remain to us as the highest
whom we know in a religious respect, and as
that one without whose presence in the heart
no perfect piety is possible. As his last work
marks the point of his furthest removal from
positive Christianity, so the 'Discourses on the
Transitory and Permanent' mark that of his
greatest approximation to it; and this is manifested at the same time in the third edition of
the 'Life of Jesus,' with regard to historically
critical questions, by his readiness to come to
an understanding with the more free-thinking

of his adversaries. Subsequently he perceived, it is true, something unsound in the frame of mind which produced this work ; he remarked that the fear of seeing himself standing so alone had thrilled through him, and had induced him to make the mistaken attempt to effect a connection between himself and those more or less believing, by means of a pathway however narrow and tottering. Still he would not contradict the friend who touchingly remarked that in his monologues he was so full of good will, and that nevertheless his convictions broke forth with inconsiderate violence.

It was a strange coincidence that about the same time in which this turn occurred in Strauss's own feelings the prospect was opened to him of using his influence as theological teacher at a university, as about the beginning of the year 1839 a professorship of theology at the Zürich University was offered him by the free-thinking Zürich government. As far as he was concerned, he found no reason in his scientific convictions for refusing an office which afforded him opportunity of indulging those convictions in

perfect freedom. But before he had had time
to enter upon his new office the government
who had nominated him found itself obliged,
by the eagerly fostered and skilfully directed
excitement of the people, to cancel its appointment, though even by this pliability it .
could not allay the storm, which burst forth
in the well-known insurrection of September
1839.

All hope was thus cut off from Strauss of
ever obtaining that position and work which
were more in harmony with his nature and his
wishes than any other, and for which he had
long shown such distinguished capability. He
made up his mind that throughout his life he
was to dispense with a thing, the privation
of which must have been an especially sore
burden to him, namely, regular professional
labour, and all the excitement, refreshment,
and satisfaction which it brings with it ; that
like an outlaw he was to find no admission
among the publicly acknowledged representatives of science, superior as he might be to
most of them ; and that with all his talent
as a teacher he could not act as such on
account of 'moral unsuitability,' for he was

never proposed or nominated even in a philosophical faculty, in more than one branch of
which he could have rendered the most important services.   He had succeeded indeed
in securing to his name a lasting importance
in the history of science, and in his youthful
years in making himself the central point
of an intellectual movement of incalculable
extent ; but for this he had heavily to atone,
inasmuch as his convictions rendered it a
duty to subject those of others to so unsparing
and irrefutable a criticism.

CHAPTER V.

In the same year in which the Zürich appointment took place, with all its excitement, its vexation, and its unfavourable issue, a second heavy blow befell our friend, namely, his mother's death. In her earlier years she had long been ill, but at the time that Strauss had first quitted his paternal home she had greatly recovered, and for ten years, though weak and delicate, she had enjoyed very tolerable health. During the last few years, however, a change had taken place, combined with a return of her former suffering condition. Repeated visits to the adjacent baths, which had before proved efficacious, were now resultless, and in March 1839 she sunk under a rapid acceleration of her malady. The paternal home therefore lost all its attraction and value for Strauss. Two years

afterwards, in April 1841, his father died
also.

All the more energetically, therefore, did
Strauss throw himself upon the only thing
that could divert him from these sad and
adverse occurrences, namely, his scientific
work. His life at Stuttgart was extremely
retired and simple. For several years he
lived alone in a small garden-house at the
back of the Charlotten-Strasse, which he had
furnished, according to his taste, in the most
unassuming manner. Besides his regular intercourse with a few intimate friends, his only
recreation was a short walk, an occasional
visit to a theatre or concert, and a short journey in summer. On the contrary, he avoided
almost timidly all larger and noisier society,
and if he did not withdraw from the visitors
whom curiosity or admiration led to him, he
nevertheless did nothing to enliven them unless he perceived a more serious interest in
his scientific investigations. He desired to
keep himself aloof from every disturbance, in
order to devote himself to work with all his
powers ; and he now turned his attention to
a task which he had already had for years

before him. We have before mentioned that even previous to his design of the 'Life of Jesus' he had sketched the plan of a work on doctrinal theology ; it had, however, given place to the 'Life of Jesus,' and for some time the idea had fallen into the background.[1] He now returned to it. He resolved to place by the side of his work on the Gospel story a similar work on the Christian system of religion, preparatory studies for which he had already partly made, originally in preparation for a lecture which was to be delivered at Zürich. Of the two volumes that formed this work the first was completed in the winter of 1839–40, and the second in the winter of 1840–41 ; the former appeared in 1840, the latter in 1841. But as Strauss's 'Life of Jesus' had become a criticism of the narratives of the life of Jesus, so his 'Doctrinal Theology' became a criticism of the Christian system of religion. The general rule of this criticism, the standard which was applied to the transmitted dogmas, was the view of modern science, and especially that of Hegel's 'Philosophy of Religion,' with

[1] Cf. page 27 and Strauss's 'Glaubensl.,' Preface.

which Strauss, at any rate at that time, agreed both as regards the speculative theology that formed its basis and also the hypothesis that in dogmas is essentially involved the scientific correctness of *representative* belief; that hence their authority and importance are determined in proportion to the harmony or contradiction in which they stand to the results of modern science, and especially to those of the Hegelian system. As, however, the critic is convinced that this proportion is not casual, but obeys an inner necessity and accords with general historical laws, the criticism of the dogma coincides in his opinion with the explanation of its historical formation and analysis, and with the history of doctrinal theology correctly understood and applied; and only by this means, so far as it is supported by the latter, can its right be indisputably proved.

'The subjective criticism of the individual,' he says, 'is a water-pipe which any boy can close for a time: criticism, objectively carried out, as it is in the course of centuries, rushes along like a roaring stream, against which all dams and sluices can effect nothing.' 'The true criticism of dogma is its history.'[1] Strauss's mode of procedure is in accordance with this. In systematic succession he examines all the principal articles of apology and dogma; at each he gives a statement of the Biblical doctrine; he shows how from this, in most cases after long wavering and with increasing expunging of anomalous opinions, rejected as heretical, the dogmas of the old, mediæval, and Protestant Church have been formed; how, however, at once in the questions which they leave unanswered, in the contrasts which they leave unreconciled, and in the contradictions which they leave unsolved, have originated the criticism of the Socinians, Arminians, Deists, Rationalists, and others, down to Schleiermacher and Hegel; he examines the various attempts that have been made to refute this criticism or to restrict it to less essential points; and in conclusion he draws from all these considerations and reflections this result, in order to establish how much of each article of faith is to be maintained when tested by the science of the present day.

[1] 'GlaubensL,' i. x. 71.

His work, as its title expressly intimates, is to exhibit ' the Christian system of religion in its historical development and in contest with modern science;' 'it is,' as he says in the Preface, 'to render that service to dogmatic science which a balance renders to a house of business;' it is 'to afford a survey of the state of dogmatic property,' and this is, in Strauss's opinion, 'all the more an urgent necessity at the present day, as the greater number of theologians indulge in the utmost illusions on the matter.' 'We estimate too lightly,' he says, 'the deduction which the criticism and polemics of the last two centuries have made from the old theological stock, and on the other hand far too highly the equivocal resources which we imagine we have found in the sentimental theology and mystical philosophy of the present day. We think we have in a great measure already gained in the enquiries still pending upon those deductions, and that we are sure of the richest gain from the newly opened shafts. It might, however, be the case that these actions might all be lost at once : and if, in addition to this, these new mines deluded

our expectations, bankruptcy would be unavoidable.'

What he here in the Preface holds out
as a possible case, we perceive in the work
itself to be his full opinion. Not merely are
the positive doctrines to which Rationalism
had long laid claim attacked by Strauss with
the double weapons of philosophical and historical criticism in a decided and severe manner, comprising all former objections; but
Strauss also turns so forcibly and plainly
against those hypotheses which the adversaries of doctrinal theology had hitherto as a
rule shared with its advocates, namely, the
personality of God, the idea of the creation,
the personal government of the world affecting each individually, and the personal existence after death, that the most general and
violent opposition could not fail to be aroused.
If in his attacks upon those positive articles
of faith he could point to a mode of thought
already widely disseminated, he had here but
few predecessors on whom he could rest; and
among these a Spinoza and a Fichte were
held in such evil repute by most persons in a
theological respect, and a Schleiermacher had

on the other hand contrived so adroitly to conceal the deductions of his Pantheism, and to blend them with the evidences of his Christian consciousness, that the greater number of his admirers scarcely perceived them, or if they did, they readily excused them as slight though always lamentable blemishes on the picture of the great man.

Strauss, on the contrary, had no such plea to screen him : he could neither plead other services rendered by him to the Church, nor had he observed any forbearance in expressing his conviction ; he had rather expressly aimed at making perfectly clear the relation in which the Christian faith stood to the science of the present day ; he was convinced, he said (i. 356), that there had been false attempts enough at reconciliation, that nothing but a separation of the opposing parties could avail, and he demanded that the man of belief should allow the man of science, and that the latter should allow the former, to pursue his own way quietly : ' if, however,' he adds, ' the over-pious should succeed in excluding us from their church, we shall regard this as an advantage.' But, in spite of this, it

was not his intention, as far as he was concerned, to sever the threads which even in his
opinion still linked them with the Church. He
disputes indeed Hegel's assertion that religion
and philosophy are identical in their substance
and only different in form, but he acknowledges that it is one and the same reason
which finds its purest expression in philosophy, but which also governs the activity of
the imagination and through the successive
series of religions leads to ever greater approximation to the truth (i. 22); and with
regard to the Christian religion especially he
says (i. 30) that it is equally onesided to
desire to see in it only the unity of the Divine
and the human or only their separation. For
far as it is removed from the monism of
modern speculation, and easily as the point
of union between the two sides can vanish
imperceptibly, it is just this same vanishing-
point to which Christianity owes its universal
historical power. The dualism of the Divine
and the human had been long before it accurately developed; the union of the two accomplished in the person of Christ had first
created new spiritual life. As the introduc-

tion to such a vast attack upon the whole structure of the Christian system of religion, this sounds placable enough : the question which Strauss thirty years afterwards could no longer answer in the affirmative : 'Are we still Christians?' he would at that time have scarcely replied to in the negative.

As a scientific and literary production the 'Doctrine of Faith' is but little inferior to the 'Life of Jesus;' on the contrary, it exhibits a still greater maturity of art. The thorough and vast knowledge of dogmatic history which in all points of any consideration is drawn direct from the primary sources, the perfect mastery of the immense material, the art with which the most important matter is sketched and the most insignificant is inserted at the right place, the steady tone of the delineation, the successful distribution of light and shade, the appropriate characterisation of every opinion and point of view, the keen perception, the able demonstration of the weak points, the defects and contradictions in dogmatic tenets and systems, the skilful use of all the available matters afforded by his predecessors, the plastic perspicuity of expression, the distinctness of arrangement and construction, the spirited vigour of the language—all these excellences are as strongly or still more strongly apparent in the ' Doctrine of Faith ' as in the earlier work ; and while the latter, especially in the monotonous repetition of the accounts of the miracles, could not avoid occasionally entering into wearisome details, the former, from the greater variety of the subject, is qualified to fascinate the reader's attention to every point from the beginning to the end. That it would, however, produce a commotion as great as that excited by the ' Life of Jesus ' was not to be expected, because the latter had robbed it beforehand of a considerable part of its effect ; and, moreover, simultaneously with the second volume of the ' Doctrine of Faith ' a work appeared in Feuerbach's ' Wesen des Christenthums ' (' Nature of Christianity') which was similar to Strauss's in substance and tendency, which was written with intelligence and spirit, and by its more popular and at the same time more radical character was still better suited to a part of the public. Nevertheless this second great work of the famous critic, as might be seen from the number and irritated tone of the replies to it, produced such an effect, and it was in itself so important, that in this respect nothing of the kind that has appeared since Schleiermacher's ' Doctrinal Theology ' can be compared with it.

After the completion of the ' Doctrine of Faith ' a pause occurred in the theological labours of its author, lasting for more than twenty years, and only broken in the year 1864 by the ' Life of Christ for the German People.' Astonishing as this may appear in a man endowed with such deep theological culture and learning, and who on his first appearance in this branch of study had won for himself a European name, it is yet conceivable from Strauss's personal character, and from the turn which his outward life as well as his theological views had taken. As Goethe composed his poems in the first place for himself, so was it also in a certain sense with Strauss, who in his sensibility and in his need of undisturbed individual development resembled the poet, whom he admired with all the warmth of a congenial nature.

He took up his pen in order to appropriate by scientific labour and artistic form aught that excited his interest, or in order to free himself by an exhaustive explanation of that which intruded itself disturbingly upon his thoughts and feelings. He required to be angry in order to write, he once said to a friend in the latter respect. The effect of his writings upon others was a secondary consideration with him, little as he was indifferent to it. His theological works had now afforded him this service as regards himself; he was settled as to his position with respect to theology; and in this settlement the positive interest which he had formerly taken in it had become so weakened that for some time it no longer acted as a stimulant. As, moreover, no professorship necessitated his continued occupation with theological questions, he had also outwardly no powerful inducement to literary work on this subject; he withdrew from personal participation in it, and followed the works of his friends as an interested spectator; but he was not to be induced to take part in them, however desired this may have

been both for the sake of the matter and the
periodicals they supplied.

Whilst he thus shrunk from publicity as
an author, he began seriously to think of
procuring for himself the basis of a satisfy-
ing human existence by a suitable domestic
life. It was not unknown to his friends that
some years before Agnese Schebest, a highly
gifted actress who had appeared at Stuttgart
as a guest, had made a deep impression upon
him not merely by the beauty of her singing
and the classical perfection of her acting, but
also by the sweetness of her nature and the
charm of her personal appearance. A second
visit afforded him opportunity of obtaining the
aim of his wishes, and in August 1842 the be-
trothal took place at Hochheim, near Heilbronn, in the presence of a few friends. The
newly-married pair resided at first in the
neighbourhood of Heilbronn, in the beauti-
fully-situated little castle at the entrance to
the village of Sontheim, and afterwards at
Heilbronn itself, where full opportunity was
afforded for intercourse with friends. Strauss
here enjoyed the intimacy of the two friends
of his youth, Märklin and Kaufmann, and

their wives, the one professor at the Gymnasium, closely connected with him by similarity
of studies and opinions ever since their university life, a man whose sound and amiable
character has been delineated with warmth
and spirit by Strauss in his well-known biography ; the other by vocation a teacher of
mathematics, but at the same time a distinguished musician, whose natural and kindly
nature expressed itself in charming vocal
compositions. In addition to these, Kerner
and his family resided at the adjacent Weinsberg ; the eldest daughter was married at
Heilbronn to Strauss's friend and physician
Dr. Niethhammer ; and besides these there
was a circle, by no means small, in which
Strauss found stimulant and recreation, especially in the regular evening meetings of the
men ; college tutors, such as Finckh and
Schnitzer, both of whom have gained reputation by philosophical works, and the latter
also by theological ones, and, on the removal
of the latter, Rümelin, now Chancellor of the
University of Tübingen ; civil functionaries,
and physicians, such as the original Dr. Sich-
erer, well known to the readers of Strauss's

'Kleine Schriften '[1] by Strauss's oration to his
memory ; merchants, such as the universally
respected Goppelt and Künzel, immortalised
jestingly by Strauss also in the ' Kleine Schrift-
en,'[2] whose constant and ready obligingness in
matters of daily life he requited on his part
by an act of literary friendship, assisting him
in the publication of an unprinted comedy by
Schiller.

But agreeable as Strauss found much in
the circumstances of his present life, he lacked
unfortunately just the two conditions of permanent happiness which were most indispen-
sable to him ; outside his home he lacked
regular professional work, and within his
home that harmony of mind for which nothing
can compensate, however valuable in itself.
The characters, the mode of education, and
the past life of Strauss and his wife, were too
dissimilar, their demands upon each other and
upon life were too different, and both were
too firmly rooted in their peculiarities. Their
marriage was not happy, and after five years
they separated by mutual agreement, though
without legal divorce. The wife repaired to

<hr>

[1] ' N.F ' 333 et seq.   [2] ' N.F.,' 476 et seq.

Stuttgart, where she had many friends, and she resided there until her death, which took place on December 22, 1870, three years previous to that of her husband. Strauss began a wandering life, from the discomfort of which he suffered not a little, without being able, however, to settle himself anywhere for more than a few years. One thing, however, he had saved from the shipwreck of his domestic life—namely, two children, whose love and whose mental development became a source of joy to him, and whose future career likewise proved in accordance with his wishes. The elder was a daughter, the younger a boy. At first, indeed, they both remained with their mother; after some years, however, Strauss took possession of them, and thus regained a considerable portion of that blessing, the full and untroubled possession of which had been denied him by fate.

It was in consequence of the circumstances just mentioned that Strauss, after having withdrawn from theology, could not for several years resolve on undertaking any larger literary work. He was not for this reason unoccupied. He read and studied

unremittingly, after his wont, but he never
arrived at writing anything; he found no subject which could have attracted him strongly
enough, and if he ever turned his attention
to one, he speedily allowed it to drop again.
The first thing by which he recalled himself
to the memory of the reading world after his
'Doctrine of Faith,' was a discourse which
he delivered to his Heilbronn friends, and
which he published with the addition of his
authorities, entitled, 'The Romanticist on the
Throne of the Cæsars, or Julian the Apos-
tate;' a spirited historical picture, but at the
same time the most acute and most striking
political satire; all the more striking the less
that could be said against the fidelity of the
historical representation, and the more tan-
gibly that in every line the parallel aimed at
forced itself upon the reader, without the
mention of any name.

Yet he had already begun a more comprehensive work. A collection of letters from
the Swabian poet Schubart, which had been
consigned to him, gave him occasion to bestow his attention more fully upon this man,
who had an especial interest for him from his

fate, as the victim of royal despotism, and
still more from his simple, good-hearted,
burly and sanguine nature, and whose poems
and history had been known to him, more
over, from his early boyhood. By his industry he succeeded in increasing from other
sources the number of letters and documents;
with the material, the impulse to turn it to
account became stronger, and thus arose
'Schubart's Life in his Letters,' as the first
of those attractive biographical delineations
which from henceforth for fifteen years almost
exclusively claimed Strauss's literary labour,
and afforded him plentiful opportunity for
proving in innocent material, remote from all
theological dispute, not only the profoundness of his research, but at the same time the
versatility of his culture, the grace and ability
of his diction, and his rare gift for artistic
arrangement. About the beginning of the
year 1848, Schubart was sent to press; but
after a few weeks the outbreak of the political
storms brought the printing to a stop, and it
was not till the following year that the work
appeared in two volumes.

The agitations of 1848 affected meanwhile

the life of our friend in other ways. When
in the March of this year the German people
passsed in review their best and most distinguished men, in order to send them to Frankfort, many thought that Strauss also would
·not be absent from the assembly, which was
to establish a new order of things for Germany. He himself, it is true, was at first not
of this opinion ; not merely, as he wrote to
me on March 27, because he could never con-
sent to a popular speech in an electoral assembly, but also because he could not perceive in himself any inclination for such a
position. This entire political movement,
with its restless ferment, was to him still too
problematic in its results for him to have any
desire to mingle in it, apart from the fact that
there was something unpleasant in it to a man
of contemplative life like himself. Yet he
could not, after all, resist the requests of his
Ludwigsburg fellow-citizens, who offered him
the candidateship of their district, and even
his disinclination to election speeches was so
far overcome that he delivered a great many
of them both at Ludwigsburg and other

places ; and had it only depended on this
town itself, there would have been no doubt
of his success. But among the country popu-
lation the reputation of unchristian tenets
stood in his way, and thus the pietistic agitation, which was supported by the majority of
the Evangelical clergy, succeeded in prevent-
ing his election, and in effecting that of a
wrong-headed fanatic, who subsequently became troublesome enough to his own party
by his eccentric fancies.

Strauss published his election speeches
under the title ' Six Theological Political
Popular Speeches ; ' and popular speeches in
the best sense they were ; true models of
luminous and generally intelligible matter,
full of political discernment, advocating the
confederation under Prussian rule, and moderation in the demands for freedom, in the
dignified tone of a man who seeks no honour
for himself, but who places his energies at
the service of the community. One effect of
the experiences made by Strauss on this
occasion was the conviction which he expresses in the preface to his popular speeches,

that direct elective proceedings hold good all
the less the more unlimited is the right of
election.

Strauss's failure at the election produced
such an excited feeling in Ludwigsburg against
his adversaries that he found himself obliged
to deliver another speech in a popular assembly for the sake of quieting the minds of the
people. All the less would his fellow-citizens
see themselves deprived of the honour of
being represented by him in the Würtemberg Diet; and as here the town had to
choose for itself alone, his election took place
with great unanimity in May 1848. When,
however, Strauss quitted Munich in September, having spent the summer there, and arrived at Stuttgart to take his place in the
Diet just opened, it was apparent only too
soon that the scruples which had prevented
him at first from accepting the post of deputy
had not been groundless. With his tempe-
rate and moderate political opinions, with his
aversion to all that was indistinct, wordy, and
tumultuous, with the critical mistrust which
was always provoked in him by the self-
satisfaction of a prevailing current of opinion,

Strauss was not the man to follow in the track of public opinion, which at that time in Würtemberg, as in the whole of South-west Germany, was inclined more and more to radicalism. He expressed this with his wonted fearlessness, both in the Diet and in public papers ; and he thus brought upon himself, as was to be expected, not merely passionate attacks from the radical party, but he perplexed many of his former friends. He was especially blamed for having expressed himself frankly in the Chamber of Deputies with regard to the licentious conduct of the press, and for having, in a very excited discussion on the shooting of R. Blum, excused the proceeding of the Austrian court-martial, and severely condemned that of the delinquent. A summons to resign his office which he consequently received from Ludwigsburg was refused by him with firmness, declaring that he had acted in obedience to the principles which he had distinctly expressed before his election, that he had never been a complier with popular opinion, and that for his own part he was indeed much inclined to give up his post of deputy, but that so long

as only a small fraction of his electors desired
that he should do so, he did not feel justified
in taking the step.

After a few weeks, however, he was
obliged to accept the conviction that he could
not longer remain in a legislative assembly
which was carried further and further on the
precipitous path of radicalism, in which he
saw himself driven to the right with his old
adversary, Wolfgang Menzel, and in all more
important divisions regularly in the minority
with nobles and prelates.   And when on
one occasion he received an undeserved call
to order for an attack upon the radicals,
he announced his retirement from the Chamber and his renunciation of all the pay
appertaining to him ; and this step he vin-
dicated in a letter to his electors, dated
December 23, 1848, by showing the hopelessness of his further influence in the community. He himself was conscious that in
so doing he had only acted in accordance
with his nature ; and if he had previously
had no high opinion of the political ability of
the masses, this idea could only be strength-
ened in him by all that he had observed and

experienced during this year. While the course of things had produced upon him in general a depressing effect, and while he found as little to praise on the one side as on the other, the democratic party inspired him with a feeling of still deeper aversion than their absolutist adversaries. 'The affairs of Germany,' he wrote on May 30, 1849, 'are in a condition which could not possibly be more lamentable. On the right and left, with princes and demagogues, there is just as little judgment as there is probity, and the threatening breach is really only delayed because the hopelessness on both sides is too great. My confession of faith in this disorder is briefly stated. I was sincerely in favour of supporting a true constitutionalism, a fixed unity with the utmost possible forbearance of existing things ; if this, however, cannot be, and if I have only to choose between the despotism of the prince and the masses, I am unhesitatingly in favour of the former. . . . You may denounce me as a heretic in consequence, but I cannot do otherwise ; the last drop of blood in me abhors the authority of demagogues as the extreme of all evils.' This was in him indisputably a well-considered political conviction ; but it was at the same time also the deep, inner aversion of his ideal, sensitive, and tender nature—of a nature which, with all its *bourgeois* simplicity, was noble in the best sense of the word—to the noise and rudeness of the public mart and to the dominion of the phraseology, the vague instincts, and the indiscreet passions of the masses.

CHAPTER VI.

LITERARY LABOURS.

STRAUSS now settled himself at Munich, and lived there again as solitary and retired as he had before done in Stuttgart, delighting in the art treasures, those of the Glyptothek especially, and limiting his intercourse to a small number of acquaintances, among whom he associated most intimately and frequently with the Orientalist Neumann and his family. In the autumn of 1851, when he took possession of his children, he removed with them, first to Weimar, where with Adolph Schöll, his old college friend, he indulged in the remembrances of the golden age of German poetry, and traced the reminiscences of Goethe, whose warm admirer he had ever been ; and in the following summer he proceeded to Cologne, where his brother resided. He obtained female assistance for the management of his small *ménage*, which he now again organised, and for the care of his children.   Their education he himself directed with love and ability ; and if one or another of his more intimate friends paid him a visit, he was sure to find in him an agreeable host.

In the early part of his Munich life Strauss had sought in vain for a suitable theme for the literary work which had again become a necessity to him.   He thought of a criticism or critical history of Christian morals;   then of a monograph on Diderot ; but the latter, on closer acquaintance with his works, failed to attract him so much as to induce him to write more about him than an article in the morning papers (May 1849) ; the former deterred him by the mass and scattered nature of the material, which he felt himself utterly inadequate to gather together.   For the collection of materials, he asserted, was unusually difficult to him, not only from his disinclination for the task, but also from his want of skill.   The only thing, he declared, which afforded him pleasure in a work was composition ;   the preparatory

compilation of material was nothing but a
sad necessity to him because it refused him
free composition; and it was all the more
sad because it caused him far more trouble
than it did others. The latter was certainly
not true. Strauss worked as a scholar very
readily and quickly, and at the same time
with unusual accuracy and profoundness; but
it may have been that his artistic nature
rendered the compilation of material, at first
formless, a more unpleasant task than to those
to whom the completeness and trustworthiness of the material is the principal thing, and
the literary form merely an accessory. It is
only, he says, when he feels the clay softening
in his hand, when he feels it readily and to
a certain extent of itself assuming the form
which his fingers are giving to it, that he is
conscious of the enjoyment of his talent; and
this moreover is certainly the talent that
peculiarly belongs to him.

Whilst he was again looking about him
for some suitable work, after having made a
few short journeys in the summer of 1849, a
painful event brought him suddenly the task
he required. This was the death of his

H

friend Märklin. He was just expecting a visit from him at Munich, when, instead, the tidings arrived that he had sunk under a rapid attack of typhus fever on October 18. The resolve was speedily made to raise a larger and more lasting monument to his friend than the necrology in the Swabian ' Mercury ' ; and in less than a year the biography was ready, which possesses all the greater value for us as it contains, with the history of Märklin's youth, that also of his biographer, as it makes the reader acquainted with the tender side of the nature of both, and affords him an insight into the way in which the two friends, amid internal and external impediments, worked their way to their scientific opinions.

That Strauss had difficulty in finding a publisher for this work marks the effect exercised by the political agitation, and by the political theological reaction upon literature, that followed it. Nor was he satisfied with the reception which it met with, so far as it undoubtedly contributed to correct the prejudices prevailing against him. He received the impression that his works were in

longer read ; he resolved therefore no longer
to write ; and for the next few years he produced in consequence only works of a smaller
size, which are to be found in the first part
of the 'Kleine Schriften' among earlier and
later productions of a similar kind.

The plan of a popular theological work in
the form of a Dictionary, which he had entertained for some time, was again relinquished.
It was not till 1854 that he again undertook a
somewhat larger task in the biography of the
poet and philologist, 'Nicodemus Frischlin,'
which appeared in the autumn of 1855.
This life of a talented man, who, in the want
of moderation that characterised him, met
with a tragic end, from a concatenation of
personal error, antagonistic attacks, and
unfortunate circumstances, forms a counter-
part to the life of the Swabian poet, who
could equally little control a nature similarly
disposed, and who presents in his history
many points of affinity with the other.

Drawn as it is with careful investigation
from a mass of published as well as unpublished and hitherto unused documents (the
difficult deciphering of which, especially of

Frischlin's letters, occasioned great labour), it
is a highly valuable contribution to the history of culture and literature in Germany in
the 16th century; and the accurate analysis
of Frischlin's different writings, which Strauss
imposed upon himself, will be all the more
welcome to those who use the book for its
scientific interest, the more difficult it is to
obtain a part of those writings, and the more
wearisome it is to read them.   But skilfully
as these abstracts are made, and little as this
work also lacks the well-known excellences
of Strauss's style, its subject was too remote
from the interest of the bulk of the public,
and the matter was in itself too heavy, for it
ever to become as popular as the other works
of its author.

The latter meanwhile, in the autumn of
1854, had quitted Cologne, which afforded
him permanently few literary resources and
too little scientific intercourse, and had settled
at Heidelberg, where he spent six years.   He
had sent his son to a school at Oehringen,
a few miles from Heilbronn, where some intimate friends resided.   His daughter was
educated in their new place of abode at

Fräulein Heidel's boarding school, in whose
principal both father and daughter found a
true friend ; and he himself in his note-book
reckons the years during which he watched
her growing up beside him under the care of
excellent beings, as among the quietly hap-
piest of his life. For his own part he returned
to his former simple bachelor life ; yet he so
arranged matters that he could lodge a friend
and could have his son with him in the holidays. As far as his work was concerned, the
University library afforded him all the assistance necessary ; and in the academical circles
he had rich opportunity for agreeable and pro-
fitable society. Strauss enjoyed friendly intercourse with most of the scientific notabilities
of the Heidelberg of that period, with Schlos-
ser, Vangerow, R. von Mohl, Haüsser, R.
Bunsen, and others, outside the University,
with the historian Weber, with the thoughtful
and free-thinking minister Zittel, and a few
others ; but he most closely attached himself
to Kuno Fischer and Gervinus, though he
did not indeed agree with the latter either
in musical, æsthetic, or subsequently in political matters, highly as he ranked him on

account of his rich and powerful mind, his
great cultivation, and his pure and noble
character : and both intimacies were all the
more valuable to him as the wives of his
friends entered with interest and intelligence
into his intercourse with their husbands. For
intercourse with cultivated women was a necessity to a nature as æsthetically inclined as
his, and endowed with the liveliest suscepti-
bility of all that was beautiful and agreeable ;
and in this society, in which he moved with
the most natural refinement, he unfolded the
tender side of his nature no less than the
brilliant qualities of his mind with a charm
which it was difficult to withstand.

In December 1856 Fischer went to Jena.
On the other hand, at about this time, Julius
Meyer (now director of the Berlin Museum)
became increasingly intimate with Strauss ;
but he also quitted Heidelberg before the
latter. Strauss's new place of abode was likewise very favourably situated for visits to and
from foreign friends, and for the summer
tours which he delighted in making with his
children in their holidays ; and the charming
neighbourhood of the place afforded oppor-

tunity for enjoyable walks and excursions.
Many things concurred to make the years
which he spent in Heidelberg both agreeable
and satisfactory.

His labours also prospered amid these
surroundings. The publication of Frischlin
was scarcely completed when he had already
begun to collect materials for the life of
Ulrich von Hütten, in which he was oblig-
ingly assisted by Böcking, who was at that
time just occupied with his excellent edition
of Hütten's works, and by these common
studies was brought into connection with him
The new work itself appeared in the autumn
of 1857 in two volumes, and in 1871 in a
second abridged form. The ' Discourses of
Ulrich von Hütten ' was added to the first
edition three years afterwards as a third part,
being a translation of all Hütten's written
discourses, with the exception of the three
earliest, accompanied with explanatory remarks. Strauss had here chosen a far more
important subject than in any of his earlier
biographical works. A man surpassed by no
other of the heroes of the Reformation age
in boldness and freedom of mind, in whose

struggles not merely the weightiest religious movement is reflected, and in great measure consummated, but at the same time also one of the weightiest scientific, political, and national movements which the history of our people has known ; a life, compared with which that of a Märklin is only like an innocent idyll, and that of a Schubart or a Frischlin like a storm in a pond compared with one in the open sea. An essential advantage to the biographer lay also in the fact that the subject in question was not merely a man of thought, but also of action ; that he possessed a fresh, vigorous nature, not without perhaps a tinge of ferocity, and that his life was connected with an historical course of events which, through exciting catastrophes and alternating failures and successes, led to an issue of agitating tragic effect. If the historian would suit himself to such material, he must handle it in a grander style than the preceding ones. And this he actually did. Basing his work on the comprehensive and accurate study of all reliable sources, Strauss sketched in his Hütten a picture of the development, career, and fate of the man ; of the

efforts, the doings, and the more important
characters of the humanistic circle to which
he belonged, and at the same time of the
violent agitation of the period in which he
exerted so powerful an influence—a picture
which attracts and fascinates us all the more,
the more warmly the personal interest of the
author in his hero becomes apparent, and the
less he conceals the fact that he desires to
bring home to the reader the parallel between
the vocation and struggles of the sixteenth and
those of the nineteenth century—a parallel
inherent in his subject, and obtruding itself
naturally from the pure historical recital—and
that he desires to address to our own age,
through Hütten, the exhortations which Hütten addressed to his own. He himself expressed this intention in the preface to the
second edition. He draws a parallel between
the circumstances under which his Hütten
first saw the light, 'the years in which Ger-
mania lay in profound weakness after the
exhaustion of an abortive childbirth, in which
great and small oppressors had again become
masters of her,' and 'the period of the con-
cordats, those slavish contracts with Rome,'

in which Austria took precedence, and all the South German governments were ready to follow. ' I cried,' he exclaims, 'is there no Hütten here ? and because there was none among the living, I undertook to revive the image of the dead, and to place it before the eyes of the German people.' ' But even now,' he adds, in the days of the Frankfort peace, ' after Germany has again an emperor, and stands at the head of the nations, Hütten is not to be invited to the triumphal feast as an idle visitor, but in order to help forward the great tasks that still lie before us, to assist us in building up the structure of German unity and freedom, and in fighting against the spiritual Rome and against the enemies to enlightenment even in Protestant Germany.' He had always conceived, he declared, Germany's power and greatness, in which he gloried, as grounded on free human mental culture, narrowed by no clergy and no ecclesiastical laws ; and, as in the war just concluded, he would have fought among the foremost against the outward foe, so he would now again fight among the foremost against the internal foes of freedom and culture.   It was this same valiant nature in his hero, this untameable desire for free human and national devolopment, weakened by no theological interests, and limited by no dogmatic hypotheses, by which Hütten attracted his biographer beyond all other great men of the time of the Reformation, and in which he felt himself inwardly allied to him. The biography of Hütten was just the subject he desired; that of Luther, which Gervinus desired should follow it, he speedily relinquished, though he had at first inclined towards it.

The tone of feeling which had imbued Strauss's mind during his occupation with Hütten's works, expressed itself with cutting severity in the ample preface which he affixed in May 1860 to his translation of the 'Discourses.' 'What would Hütten say to our present age?' he asks; and he then proceeds to a review of the Catholicism, and to a still more thorough review of the Protestantism, of the present day, which passes into a harsh condemnation of modern theology and Church matters. Of no party, Strauss here declares, does one like to say the sincere truth. In reality, no cultivated man, whether clergyman

or layman, believes any longer in the dogmas
of the Church, whether he is conscious of it or
not ; no more believes in any of the New Testament miracles, from the supernatural conception to the Ascension. What use therefore
in prevarication ? Why indulge hypocrisy to
others and to ourselves ? Why not openly
speak the truth ? Why not mutually confess
that we can perceive nothing in the Biblical
stories but fiction and truth, and in the dogmas
of the Church nothing but significant symbols ;
but that we remain attached with unalterable
reverence to the moral value of Christianity,
and to the character of its founder, so far as
the human form is recognisable amid the
accumulation of miracles in which its first
biographers have enveloped it ? Yet can we,
after all, venture to call ourselves Christians ?
' I know not,' answers Strauss, ' but does it
then depend on the name ? This know I,
that we shall then only again become true,
honest, and undistorted, and therefore better
men than hitherto. We shall remain Protestants ; in fact, we shall then only be true
Protestants.'

With this tone of feeling it cannot excite

surprise if a plan which he had conceived
about the beginning of the year 1858, soon
after the completion of Hütten's biography,
of writing a series of biographies of German
poets—Klopstock, Lessing, Wieland, Herder,
Goethe, and Schiller—was speedily relinquished. Klopstock, as he soon found, was
not sympathetic to him.; the one, however, of
his contemporaries who was so to the highest
degree, and whose portrait we should above
all have wished to possess from his masterly
hand, was just at that time the subject of a
biography by A. Stahr, whose work satisfied
Strauss in the main matter, and seemed for
the present to render his own superfluous.
He therefore let the matter rest, after having
prepared two fragments on Klopstock, one of
which he published in 1862, with various
other small works in the first part of his
' Kleine Schriften ;' and the other, and far
larger one, the pleasing and instructive ' History of Klopstock's Youth,' he published in
1866, in the second part of the same work.
With regard to the other contents of these
two collections, as they have not been hitherto
touched upon, we may mention the study

upon A. W. Schlegel,[1] written in the year
1849 ; the article upon King William of Würtemberg ;[2] and the six political and three
non-political ' Discourses' written in the years
1863 and 1865.[3] It was, however, not merely
disinclination to occupy himself for any length
of time with Klopstock, and with any work
referring solely to the history of literature,
which made him so speedily stop short in his
intended biographies of the poets to return to
Hütten in the translation of the ' Discourses ;'
but it was at the same time the re-awakening
of an inclination which from time to time he
had indeed imagined had wholly died within
him.   In his Hütten he had again ap-
proached the theological questions which he
had never entirely lost sight of ; and the
longer his mind wandered within their range,
the stronger was the attraction which they
again exercised over him.   Even in the preface to the ' Discourses,' the strength of this
newly-awakened theological interest is not to
be mistaken ; and the point in the direction
in which it was first to turn is plainly pointed

---

[1] I. 122 et seq.   [2] 1864 ; II. 270 et seq.
[3] II. 381 et seq.

out when, alluding to the five-and-twenty
years' jubilee of the 'Life of Christ,' he proceeds to examine the subsequent course and
present position of the investigations which
it had prompted, and declares in conclusion
that the work was not laid aside, but was
steadily advancing.

The same tendency of mind is exhibited
in the studies and reflections in the work on
Hermann Samuel Reimarus (1862). Strauss
here depicts to us with his usual masterly
power his most remarkable predecessor in the
eighteenth century, and he gives a highly
instructive and accurate account of that work
of Reimarus (still unpublished as a whole)
which Lessing took from the Wolfenbüttel
fragments, at the same time exhibiting the
relation between the Biblical criticism of
Reimarus and his own. In these explanations we find him again decidedly in theological waters ; his ' Reimarus ' was an inci-
dental production in his preparatory labours
for a work in which he was steering back towards the investigations which had first made
his name famous, namely, ' The Life of Christ
treated for the German People.'

CHAPTER VII.

THEOLOGICAL WORKS.

WHILST he had himself withdrawn from theological matters, the investigations to which he had given so powerful an impetus had not been standing still; and if, generally speaking—so far as they are scientifically to be taken into consideration—they moved on the same fundamental basis of historical criticism as his own, a tendency was nevertheless given to them by his teacher Baur, which in its treatment as well as in its results served to complete and correct his own investigations. He had been among the first to aim at a separation of the non-historical elements from the Gospel narratives; but the question how this non-historical element had found its way into them he had satisfied himself with answering in the manner before described (page 43), by referring it to the unintentionally-devised legends and the mythical imagination of the earliest Christian communities.

Baur found himself by no means satisfied either with this answer or with the manner in which Strauss had proceeded in his criticism. He believed that every investigation of the contents of the Gospel writings ought to be preceded by the investigation of these writings themselves, of the tendency which biassed them, and of the period and circumstances of their composition. In this investigation he did not, however, desire to limit himself to the Gospels; and in carrying it out he had not originally started with them, but with the Epistles of St. Paul and the Acts of the Apostles; he extended it rather to all the New Testament writings, and even beyond these to the entire Christian literature of the first two centuries; and whilst he combined with this all that the earliest Church history and that of doctrinal theology afforded him, he arrived at the opinion that the development of Christianity at this period, from the fundamental antagonism of Judaism and Paulinism, had been accomplished amid many internal struggles and manifold attempts at reconciliation, and that the different phases of these events are marked out to us by the writings which we possess both within and without our New Testament works. In this process the Gospels also have each their assigned place; and in the fourth Gospel especially we perceive the work which in a dogmatic point of view brought this to a relative conclusion, presenting in the most complete and ideal form the theological opinions of the Christian Church as they existed about the middle of the second century; for this very reason, however, this Gospel, less than all the others, is to be regarded as an authentic source of Gospel history, but throughout only as a free composition guided by dogmatic principles. If by this all that men had hitherto believed they knew with regard to the Founder of Christianity was thus in great measure called in question, Baur sought on the other hand to place Christianity itself in the light of a truly historical examination, exhibiting not merely in the Jewish, but also in the Hellenist and Hellenistic world the civilised conditions from

which it had emanated as the natural fruit of
the previous development of mind.[1]

Strauss had followed these investigations
and the writings in which they were conducted by Baur and his disciples with great
interest from the first, and to many questions
of importance he had given his assent; Baur's
'Treatise on the Gospel of St. John,' for instance, which he highly admired, had at once
produced the impression on him that it had
solved the mystery of this most remarkable
Gospel. Not merely were the books and
treatises of the Tübingen school now again
examined, and this more completely than
hitherto, but every study was made which
seemed to be necessary for the renewed treatment of the subject. About the beginning
of the year 1864 the new 'Life of Jesus'
appeared, and in the same year, in spite of
the size of the first edition, a second was
required. The difference both in form and
purport between it and the former work of
the same name was not inconsiderable. If

[1] I have more fully expressed myself on this point and on
its connection with Strauss's 'Leben Jesu' in my 'Vorträgen
und Abhandl.,' p. 284 et seq. ; 322 et seq. ; and 412 et seq.

the one was designed exclusively for theologians, the other was addressed expressly to the German people; and as Strauss stated in the dedication to his deceased brother, he had also those in view who, without any learning of their own, have manifested interest and freedom of mind in investigations of the kind. The range of his work was therefore somewhat smaller, and the learned material which was placed before the reader was more limited than in the first work; still it was ever a far too profound and accurate scientific investigation for it to claim, in spite of its lucid and pleasing style, a popularity of the same kind as that obtained by Renan's lighter work, which appeared at the same time, with its florid language, its sentimental rhetoric, and its romantic colouring, and completion of the historical course of events.

In its purport, the second ' Life of Jesus ' went essentially beyond the first. While the latter was chiefly limited to the question as to the correctness of the Gospel narratives, and to the authentication of their non-historical elements, and had only added in the concluding dissertation a criticism of Ecclesi-

astical Christology and its more recent trans-
formations, Strauss, it is true, entirely excluded
these dogmatic discussions from the plan of
his second work ; on the other hand, however,
he entered far more comprehensively into the
historical task of the Gospel criticism than in
the first work. Agreeing with Baur in all
essential points, he investigated the question
of the origin, the connection, and the character of our four Gospels; he supplemented
his criticism, to which it had not without
justice been objected that it left off at a
merely negative result, with a sketch of the
' Life of Jesus,' which was intended to establish what could be stated with more or less
certainty after the withdrawal of the non-
historical traditions, with regard to the person, teaching, ministry, intentions and fate of
the Founder of our religion ; and only after
this positive statement of the historical element which lies at the foundation of the
Gospel records, he introduced, in harmony
with his former work, the criticism of the
non-historical traditions and the investigation
of their origin and formation.

As regards its form, this part of the work,

in which Strauss enters with the greatest ease
and ability into critical discussions long familiar to him, is certainly the most perfect.
Newer material is, however, afforded by the
preceding positive investigation respecting
the person and the history of Christ ; and if
we can for once reconcile our minds to the
removal of all that is miraculous from this
history, we shall be obliged to confess that it
is here handled not merely very circumspectly
and profoundly, but also with the reverence
due to it.   Even on the point in which his
mythical interpretation had been most found
fault with—namely, the Resurrection of Christ,
he had already in ' Reimarus' [1] expressed himself more reasonably than could have been
expected from one who was not able to admit
of a miracle here any more than elsewhere.
For as he constantly affirmed that a decep-
tion was in this case out of the question, and
that it was not the visions of Christ which
produced the disciples' belief in the Resurrection, but that these were far rather themselves a result of this belief, a form which it
assumed to their own consciousness, so he

[1] P. 281 et seq.

declares, with regard to its significance, that it was, it is true, a delusion, 'yet a delusion comprising within itself a vast amount of truth. That not the visible, but the invisible, not the earthly, but the heavenly, not the flesh, but the spirit, is the true and essential matter, and the truth which has transformed the history of the world, first became the common property of mankind in the form of the belief in the Resurrection of Christ.'

In the 'Life of Jesus,' it is true, we find no equally distinct declaration on this point; but of this work also it must be allowed that it unreservedly acknowledges the Founder of the Christian religion in His human greatness, and setting aside other passages, we have only to compare the section on the religious consciousness of Christ [1] in order to convince ourselves how little the author fell short of a due understanding of the grandeur and purity of a religious character.

Two smaller works followed the 'Life of Jesus,' one of which was written in the same year and the other in the following spring, namely, 'The Christ of Faith and the Jesus

[1] P. 204 et seq.

of History,' and 'The Halves and the Wholes.' The first of these works is a criticism of Schleiermacher's 'Lectures on the Life of Jesus' which had just appeared ; the second is a controversial treatise directed against Schenkel and Hengstenberg. That the criticism should prove throughout luminous and convincing was to be expected beforehand. It surprises us more when, in the polemical treatise, we see the orthodox fanatic, his old and passionate adversary, sharply as his apologetic extravagances are proved, personally treated by Strauss far more gently than a theologian who in his opinions approximated to him so closely, and who thus had drawn upon himself such violent enmity from the orthodox party, as Schenkel had done.

But in the case before us, personal and real grounds concurred to give this tone of unsparing acrimony to his controversy. On the one side he entertained a profound repugnance to all ambiguity and all false reconciliation in scientific matters ; he could not endure any mitigation of his own regardlessly energetic criticism, and he received it as a

personal offence that Schenkel's ' Charakter-
bild Jesu ' should be placed on a level with
his book in public discussions. On the other
hand he could not forgive his adversary for
having formerly come forward against Kuno
Fischer, while at the same time he was himself provoked by the misplaced zeal with
which Schenkel's friends endeavoured to separate their cause from his, and by injurious
attacks upon him to place themselves in a
better light. It is not without interest to
hear Strauss at the conclusion of his polemical treatise declare, with reference to the
question before discussed—namely, belief in
the Resurrection of Christ—that Christianity
in its original form perishes, it is true, with
this fact, and indeed has already perished
with it.

If we ask whether Christianity itself is so
intertwined with this form, or rather with this
aggregate of its forms, that they cannot be
surrendered without a renunciation of Christianity, it is indeed but a strife about words
and names, the deciding of which still lies in
the distance. ' That which, however, may be
established, is this : If Christianity be truth,

it cannot require untruth for its support ; whatever in it needs such a support is not its truth, but is the error contained in it ; what is left, when these supports fall, with the errors they uphold—we believe, however, that somewhat, and not indeed a little, is left—that alone is the truth of Christianity.   In this itself,' and with this dilemma Strauss here concludes, ' lies the choice, whether it will stand with its truth, contracted as it becomes, or will perish with its untruth, while imagining that it cannot part with it.'

CHAPTER VIII.

THE CONFESSION OF FAITH.

WHEN Strauss was engaged on the works just mentioned, he had already long quitted Heidelberg. He had at first in the autumn of 1860 gone for some time to Berlin, in order to consult Gräfe about a troublesome complaint in his eyes, a double sight, which was removed by means of an operation, and he had then removed his place of abode to Heilbronn, in order to have his son, while he was attending the gymnasium there, under his own immediate care; his household affairs were managed by his daughter, who had meanwhile grown up, and he thus after long privation enjoyed in a manner most delightful to him the comfort of a home of his own with his two children, which gave occasion moreover for more lively intercourse with intimate friends. ´When, however, in November 1864,

his daughter married Herr Heusler, Director
of Mines in Bonn (now Chief Director of the
Mining Department), whilst his son had gone
a year previously to the University, he gave
up his abode at Heilbronn, and went for the
winter to Berlin, where he had no lack of
older and younger friends ; among those with
whom he here chiefly associated, in addition
to Vatke, was his Swabian fellow-countryman
and old pupil, Berthold Auerbach.

During the spring and summer he visited
by turns Heidelberg, Baden-Baden, and Munich, and stayed with his daughter at Biebrich
and afterwards at Bonn; and at last, in the
autumn of 1865, after long wavering, he took
up his abode at Darmstadt, which, in addition
to its library and theatre, recommended itself
to him from its freedom from noise and from
the woods in its vicinity. Here he remained
for seven years, until the autumn of 1872,
with the exception of the winters of 1867 and
1868, which he passed in Munich, in intercourse with his friend Julius Meyer, and occasional lengthy visits to his daughter and the
grandchildren with which she had gladdened
him ; and in the summer, as a rule, a few

weeks which he spent, for his health's sake, most gladly in her society, on the banks of Lake Constance, or in some other suitable place. Standing alone, as he now again did, he lived all the more retired as the circle of his acquaintances in his new abode was at first very limited ; so much so, that he himself remarked, on a visit to his daughter, that he had so thoroughly given himself up to the enjoyment of her filial tenderness, and her firmly established domestic happiness, that it would require some time before he could accustom himself again to his solitude. In time, however, nearer personal relations formed themselves round him ; and the intercourse he enjoyed from 1867 with Her Royal Highness, Princess Alice of England, the consort of Prince Louis of Hesse, was of special importance to him. Through her he became also personally acquainted with her Imperial Highness, the Crown Princess of Prussia and Germany ; and the gracious interest which the two intelligent and noble ladies showed in him to the end was among the brightest and most gratifying experiences of his later life, and cast a ray of light, as

he gratefully boasted, even into his sick-
room.

Even in Darmstadt he continued his
scientific and literary employments in his
wonted manner, although the state of his eyes
was a hindrance to him, especially in the
winter. He had from the first a work in
view which was intended to exhibit definitively
his theological and philosophical convictions,
a confession of faith as he also called it ; and
with this idea he studied whatever seemed
suitable to his purpose in the modern philosophical literature with which he was still
unacquainted. Nevertheless some time
elapsed before this idea had assumed a defi
nite form in his mind, and as no other greater
task lay just then before him, a pause of
several years occurred in Strauss's literary
labours, which was only interrupted in 1866
by the second part of the ' Kleine Schriften,'
before alluded to (p. 105) ; and when he again
undertook something new, it was not even
then at first the proposed ' Confession of
Faith,' but a biographical production, which,
however, stands in similar relation to it, as
the work on Reimarus had before done to

the second revision of the 'Life of Jesus.'
As he had preceded this work by a monograph on a German predecessor of the
eighteenth century, he found himself now
impelled to a thorough study and a mono-
graphical delineation of the man who at the
same time, in France, had expressed and influenced with more brilliant talent and success
than any other the position of French enlightenment with regard to Christianity—
namely, *Voltaire.* If the subject of this work
was suggested to him by the whole tendency
of his studies at that time, its form was determined by its special personal purpose. The
six lectures on Voltaire are real lectures which
were written for the Princess Alice, and were
listened to by her; and with reference to this
circumstance, when they were published, they
were dedicated to her; and this their purpose
was at all events not without its influence in
leading their author, without detracting from
their historical profoundness, to surpass himself in the spirited eloquence and lucid perspicuity of his style, and to give us in them
the most perfect biographical work of art
which our literature possesses, after Goethe's

Truth and Fiction.   As such they have been acknowledged by the reading world ; the first edition had scarcely appeared (1870) than a second became immediately necessary, and this was followed in 1872 by a third, a success which could only be enjoyed by a work upon the French poet and critic, with whom few at the present day in Germany are acquainted, in consequence of such unusually attractive handling.

No small approval was enjoyed by a little work which suggested itself to Strauss through the outbreak of the Franco-German War.   While, from the experiences he had made in 1848, he had abstained from any attempt at personal political activity, still, as may be readily supposed, he followed the course of public affairs with an interest, the traces of which may be perceived in his writings.   Thus, for instance, the pretty lecture upon Lessing's 'Nathan' (1864) had a political motive; and with this Strauss opened a series of lectures which were delivered at his desire in 1861 at Heilbronn, in behalf of the German fleet.   When in 1863 the new phase in the destinies of Germany began with the Schleswig-Holstein War, he expressed himself in the political ' Discourses ' [1] upon the position and vocation of Germany ; and if he could not, as is readily conceivable, under the existing state of things, overcome the general mistrust felt by the Liberal party against the leader of the Prussian policy, his conviction of the vocation of Prussia in Germany is not at any rate to be doubted. This mistrust was brilliantly refuted by the year 1866 ; and Strauss belonged to those who welcomed with the most untroubled delight the new turn of affairs in his country, and looked confidently towards the future to repair the deficiencies which still adhered to the work of that year. When the decisive contest of 1870 promised to bring this hope nearer its goal, he addressed a letter in the Augsburg ' Allgemeine Zeitung' to Ernst Renan, who in a letter suggested by his ' Voltaire' had expressed his opinion to him also with regard to the war, and he here made the attempt to explain to the French scholar, and at the same time to the world generally, the recent political and national development of our people ; the true causes of the war,

[1] See above, p. 105.

K

and Germany's right in it; and when Renan's reply, and a contemporaneous article by him in the 'Revue des Deux Mondes,' showed how little even one of the most intelligent and just thinking of the French, even after the days of Gravelotte and Sedan, was able to conceive the true position of things, and to rise above the prejudices, self-delusions, and pretensions of his nation, he followed his first letter by a second, in which, with great perspicuity, he represented the state of the case, and proved the right and the necessity for Germany to take back the provinces wrung from her in the seventeenth century. The favourable reception awarded to these two letters, which he published separately, together with a translation of Renan's, under the title 'War and Peace,' contributed to induce him to carry out the idea of re-publishing his 'Hütten' in a more popular form, as has been already mentioned at page 98.

Had our friend concluded his literary career with these works, we should have received from them the impression that, after the violent contests which he had provoked in his earlier years by the boldness of his theological criticism, his career had at last found a conciliatory conclusion in the lively concern he took in the political and national interests of his people. But to himself something would have been lacking to the completeness of his own life ; he would have had the feeling of having a task imposed upon him by his convictions, had he not freely spoken out all that lay upon his heart with regard to our present age, and had he not attempted to fashion into a whole the views which resulted from his scientific opinions.

The idea of such a work he had, as we have already seen, long entertained, and had made studies for it. In 1871 he entered upon its execution, and in October 1872 appeared 'The Old and New Faith: a Confession.' How he himself intended this work to be regarded, and that he was as much in earnest in the 'Confession' as his pious adversaries could alone be in the confessions and evidences so familiar to them, he has thus expressed in a dedicatory letter which he appended to his book.[1]

[1] This letter, addressed in Latin to an old friend of his youth, was published soon after Strauss's death in the Vienna

'I have made the confession of faith,' he says, 'which God has ordered me to make. I have delivered my discourse from the beginning to the end. If I now die, it can no longer be said that I owe aught at my death to any age and to any nation. What I had I have given to them; what was still left

Neuen Freien Presse (1874, March 5, No. 3,421), in an interesting article on the last year and a half of his life, which is to be recommended to the notice of all future biographers of Strauss. I insert it here as a specimen of the excellent Latin which was at the command of its author :—
'Venit tandem, amice, nec se diutius exspectari patitur libellus meus novus, imo, nisi præsagia animi fallunt auctorem, novissimus. Sentio vires, non tam ingenii quam corporis, labare et serena mente dictum illud repeto :
'Vixi, et quem cursum dederat fortuna, peregi. Quod injunctum mihi a numine erat ut profiterer neque homines celarem, professussum : sermonem quasi meum a primo jam usque ad ultimum verbum recitavi. Non ultra dices, quando moriar, debitorem me æqualium aut nostralium esse moriturum. Quæ habebam, cum eis communicavi : libellus hic quidquid supererat continet. Sed dices forsitan, multa me omisisse, plura quam æquum sit in disputatione mea desiderari. Multa, fateor, omisi ; sed non negligens, sed sciens ac volens. Res acu tangere, non penitus pertractare volui. Non docere ex cathedra, sed quasi libere conversari cum lectoribus mihi proposui. Se non satis eruditos a me esse si lectorum aliqui fortasse querentur, dolebo ; sed si scintillas ex hominum animis undique excussisse hoc libello non dicar, tum demum male me scripsisse concedam. Ceterum de eventu libelli ecce me egregie securum. Quod debebam ut poteram fui : jam fiat quod potest ; et sic debuisse fieri mihi persuadendo acquiescam. Ni vero, amicissime, vale et me amare perge.'

unsaid this work contains. . . . I have not
the slightest anxiety as to its fate. What I
had to do I have done to the best of my
ability; happen now what will, I shall quiet
myself in the conviction that it must have
happened.'

Anyone who has known him and had intercourse with him, especially in the latter
years of his life, will not doubt the sincerity
of his statement. He intended in this work
to make, as it were, his theological and philosophical testament, and to give the result
of the labours and studies of his life both
for himself and for others; and that this
result might exhibit itself as purely as possible, and that no element foreign to its true
purpose might hinder the vast influence of
his work; that, as he wrote to me on October 17,
1872, and as he also expressed himself in the
'Neuen Freien Presse,' 'he might not again
fall into the error of scholarly dulness which
had proved the ruin of his new 'Life of Jesus,'
he desired to disencumber it as much as possible from all substantial matter, and 'for
this once to work freely and as it were without compass and rule.'

This he did with such masterly power; he so completely eradicated every trace of the labour which his work had caused him, and of the study which it had cost him, and he purified his rich material to such transparent clearness, that this his last principal work, considered as a work of art, occupies an equally distinguished position among his philosophical and theological writings as ' Voltaire' does among his biographical. He himself, it is true, was aware that what his work thus obtained in freshness and vigour must have been unavoidably purchased at the loss of completeness and symmetry; that a line of battle of such vast extent could not at the same time have been drawn up deeply; that weak points must have been left; and that only the daring feat of the whole could compensate for this deficiency in its parts. As such a point of weakness, which, in spite of repeated retouching, could never wholly satisfy him, he designated in one of his letters the beginning of the fourth section on Morals. ' Here,' he writes immediately after the appearance of the work, ' a couple of solid beams have still to be inserted, and if you could supply me with a few oak, or even pine stems, you would deserve my sincere thanks. The work touches me too closely for me to take counsel with myself respecting it.'

If, however, we are inclined on this account to regard . it as the hastily written production of a passing tone of feeling, we are decidedly in error. He is, indeed, fully justified when he guards against this in the lines found among the papers he has left behind :—

'Carelessly it seems expressed,
  Though not carelessly achieved ;
Within a few weeks is compressed
  That which was through years conceived.'

The subject of the work at present under our consideration is too well known and is too fresh in remembrance for it to be necessary for us to enter more accurately into it here. The first two of the four sections into which it is divided gather together with great skill, clearness, and conciseness the essential purport of the objections which Strauss had opposed in his earlier writings, not merely to the positive Christian dogmas and historical narratives which form their bases, but

also to the belief in the personality of God
and the personal existence after death,
strengthening these objections here and
there with further remarks ; and from this
is drawn the conclusion, that, of the two
questions, 'Are we still Christians ?' and
'Have we still any religion ?' the first is
simply to be answered in the negative, and
the second, on the other hand, is, it is true,
generally speaking, to receive an affirmative
reply, but nevertheless only so far is the
name of religion not refused to the feeling
of an absolute dependence, and to that which
arises from it, submission to the course of the
world, inner freedom, and joyfulness of mind,
when that feeling, as in Schleiermacher, refers
to the greatness, perfection, legality, and ra-
tionality of the system of the world instead
of a personal God.

The positive side of this criticism of the
religious opinions hitherto existing, is afforded
by the two following sections, which unfold
the distinguishing features of the theory
of life, which, according to the author's
opinion, rests upon the position of the
science of the present day. His guiding

point is the tracing back of the world to its natural causes, and of human action to its natural motives. For the first of these tasks Strauss makes use especially of two modern theories of physical science—that which Kant and Laplace advanced with regard to the origin of the solar system, and that which Darwin brought forward with regard to the origin of organic nature and of its various kinds ; expressly, however, he admits with respect to the latter, that it is after all most defective, leaving infinitely much unexplained, and among these many principal and cardinal points ; that it aims rather at future possible solutions than itself furnishing them. The doubt, however, that in this way he allows to fall upon materialism deters him all the less, as for his own part he believes materialism and idealism are only the mutually compensating forces required for the just theory of life, both of which have their common adversary in dualism ; in a similar manner as he observes a just medium (p. 218. 143) between the kindred contrast of the mechanical and teleological interpretations of nature, on the one side agreeing with the Darwinian

idea that blind natural instinct can produce
what is suited to its purpose, and on the other
side according with the statement that, if the
world is not the work of an absolutely wise
and judicious personality, it is at any rate the
workshop of judiciousness and wisdom. In
his contemplation of human life he starts with
the conviction that all moral action is a self-
determination of the individual, according to
the idea of the species ; it consists in this,
that it is realised in the man himself and is
recognised in others ; and with this is connected a discussion of the most important
moral, social, and political questions, to which
even adversaries can scarcely refuse the praise
of a sound moral judgment and a pure and
noble spirit. Two 'supplementary notices'
upon our great poets and musicians touched
upon æsthetic grounds, and no susceptible
reader will follow the author's reflections without rich enjoyment and stimulated interest.

Such a work could not fail to excite the
greatest sensation. The name of its author,
the extent and importance of the questions it
involved, the profusion of ideas, the keenness
of the criticism, the clear, brilliant, and spirited

style, all combined to produce an attraction
which was however counterbalanced in most
by the repulsive ·effect of a theory of life
which they could only consider as reprehen-
sible and comfortless. And it was not merely
the decided and fundamental adversaries of a
free theological criticism who received this
impression from Strauss's last work ; but even
from those on whose moderation and imparti-
ality he had some reason to reckon, even from
men of liberal views, both theologically and
politically, he found, as a rule, but little ap-
probation. Readily as they had submitted to
the criticism of positive dogmas, they could
not forgive him the cutting denial of the question, ' Are we still Christians?' nor the lively
and regardless attacks upon convictions which
rationalism and enlightened opinions could
all the less willingly renounce, as they had
already cast overboard so many and such important fragments of the original stock of
dogmas. But even many of his hitherto more
decided friends had their scruples at this new
venture. Was this criticism of the old Faith
with its negative results competent on all
points ? And admitted it were so ; is *Chris-*

tianity in its profoundest nature and influence irrevocably linked to Christian *dogmatics*, and is religion allied to distinct dogmas ? Must we renounce the idea of God as such if we become convinced of the insufficiency of the conceptions which we have formed in our own mind of God, from the analogy of the human nature ? Does not the unity of the world ever pre-suppose one cause at work, and can we be satisfied to regard as such the blindly acting power of matter, if we, as Strauss himself says, 'must attribute to the cause that which we see in the effect,' and if in the effect, as he likewise admits, an infinite exuberance of spiritual life has lain from eternity, and will rest for all eternity to come ? And is not the case similar in the narrower sphere of human consciousness ? Is the question between materialism and spiritualism so insignificant that we should venture to divest ourselves of its decision ? Is there any prospect, on the other hand, of explaining the manifestations of consciousness by the physical organism as such, or can the impossibility of this explanation be proved ? These and similar questions might well deter many who had gone a great way with Strauss from following him on the last step. A few undoubtedly, however, assumed this position, because even without more accurate investigation they were convinced of the inadmissibility of his position. The reception which his work received afforded therefore a peculiar spectacle. On the one side it excited the most universal interest; in six months six large editions appeared, to which a seventh has now been added; a success which has indeed never attended any other theological or philosophical work in Germany. On the other hand, the public discussions of the work were almost without exception disapproving; and if the horror of the orthodox adversaries was mitigated by the sense of satisfaction that the dreaded critic had now fully unmasked himself in all his reprehensibility, the representatives of average theological liberalism pressed forward almost still more eagerly than the orthodox opponents to renounce all compromising association with a man whose opinions certainly went so far beyond their own, that he could from henceforth no longer reckon on their concurrence.

And, as it generally happens, this was not
always done with the tact and consideration
which a man like Strauss might have claimed.
Men who in mind, knowledge, and achieve-
ment stood still further below him than in
years, ventured to readjust his sketch as though
he were a boy ; what his 'confession' as such
denoted with regard to himself, what assistance it could afford to the science of the present time by the questions it suggested and
the tasks it proposed, was not taken into consideration.   Among those however who were
most qualified to appreciate it justly, few at
first would or could take up the sword ; and
those who thoroughly examined it were
obliged to confess that, in spite of the free and
apparently slight treatment of the subject, it
involved the refutation of long and laborious
thought, which was not to be set aside by a
few hastily-written journal articles, but the
criticism of which, if it was to be conclusive,
demanded nothing less than a new system of
metaphysics.   Thus it was that Strauss's last
work, like his first, so far as may be drawn
from the public expressions of opinion, was
just as eagerly attacked as it was read, and

that in this contest he now in his old age stood as much alone as he had done at the beginning of his career.

But this he had not now expected. First and foremost in his work, the expression of his own conviction had been of importance to him ; his critics could find in it, almost without exception, only one culpable attack upon their own opinions. This, perhaps, coolly considered, could not have greatly surprised him. But such a consideration was little to be expected from him at the first moment. Many as were the contests which he had challenged during his life with the utmost intrepidity, and which he had maintained with the greatest scientific courage, he had nevertheless, finely strung and sensitive as he was by nature, never become so storm-proof as not to look forward with suspense to the reception of his works, and not to be passionately excited by the attacks which they brought upon him. He was deeply grieved, and it required some time before he could regain his calm composure. But, as he writes to a friend,[1] ' The evil moment to him was at

---

[1] Neuen Freien Presse.

all times only that when he heard the cry,
The Philistines be upon thee, Samson! and
the hair of his head had not yet grown
again.'

In the present case this happened quickly
enough. At the second edition of his work
he encourages himself with the martial
words : —

> Up! time-worn warrior, hush thy fears,
>   And gird thy loins for strife !
> Fierce contest marked thy early years,
>   And it shall close thy life.

And on the last day of the year 1872 he
finished a concluding address, which was at
the same time to serve as a preface to the
fourth and all succeeding editions of his work;
a written defence of his opinions, which by its
dignified and moderate bearing, by the noble
modesty with which the celebrated author
speaks of himself and his achievements, and
by the calm and cultivated tone in which he
answers injurious reproaches, must have produced a reconciling and softening impression
upon many who were hostile towards him on
account of his ' Confession.' All that he had
done in his work, he says, was only to gather
together thoughts which had long been ac-

knowledged separately. He had intended in it to bring to the consciousness of those like-minded with himself what we possess and what we do not possess. In placing before them the present state of our opinions and knowledge, of our incentives and tranquillising influences, he had desired at the same time to draw attention to the points in which these were still deficient. No dispute with those of contrary opinions, nothing but an understanding with those of like mind, had been his intention. Of such he had the right to demand by his ' Confession ' that they should live up to their convictions, not accommodating themselves to other opinions, nor belonging to any Church ; and in spite of all invectives, he remained convinced that in this ' Confession ' he had done a good work, and had gained the thanks of a less prejudiced future. ' The time of agreement,' he says, in conclusion, 'will come, as it came to the " Life of Jesus," only that this time I shall not live to see it.'

CHAPTER IX.

ILLNESS AND DEATH.

THE presentiment expressed in these concluding words was only too soon to be realised.
Strauss had left Darmstadt in October 1872,
in order to return to his Swabian home. He
had first thought of Stuttgart, where his son,
soon after his successful return from the war,
had received an appointment as military physician; finally, however, he had preferred his
old Ludwigsburg avenues to the noise of the
capital, which during the last thirty years had
not a little increased. Here he arranged a
small abode not far from the railway station.
But soon after the beginning of the year 1873
there appeared foretokens of a malady which
proclaimed itself in more decided symptoms
as the spring advanced. It seemed at first a
disorder of the bowels, which it was hoped
would be remedied by Karlsbad; but when

he returned from thence at the end of May, there was no improvement, and his disorder appeared rather on the increase. Constant pains in the back and limbs impeded his walking, sitting, or lying, and deprived him of sleep. A rapid diminution of strength excited apprehension. While Strauss had hitherto looked younger than he was—his head thickly covered with brown hair, by degrees verging into grey; his face thin, as was its wont, but healthy and fresh in com-plexion; and his movements quick and vigorous, and only impeded by his short-sightedness—he now rapidly became the old man. I had last seen him in September 1872. When, eleven months afterwards, I visited him in his illness, I was alarmed at the visible traces of his great decline of strength; and I could no longer feel doubtful of his own just estimate of his condition when he, before by letters, and now by word of mouth, expressed the conviction that his life was only to be reckoned by months. His son treated him from Stuttgart, with the as-sistance of Elsässer, the director of the pro-vincial board of health, an older physician of

some eminence, who had been a college friend
of Strauss, and who died a few weeks after
him.   The nursing of the sick man was undertaken with devotion and care by Caroline
Gerber, an old servant and friend of the
family, whom he highly valued on account
of her attachment and trustworthiness.   But
no medical skill or nursing could check the
progress of the disease, which from a tumour
in the bowels seemed to proclaim itself of a
cancerous character, though its true nature
could not be fully ascertained until after his
death.   The suffering and pain increased, his
strength sank still lower ; and though at one
time there seemed a pause in the progress of
the malady, the hope encouraged by it was
speedily disappointed.

But in these very sufferings the mental
greatness and moral strength of the sufferer
proclaimed their most glorious victory.   He
was fully aware of his condition.   With un-
shaken firmness he adhered to the convictions
which he had openly acknowledged in his
last work, and he never for a moment re-
pented having written them.   But with these
convictions he met death with such repose,

and with such unclouded serenity of mind,
that it was impossible to leave his sick-room
without that impression of a moral sanctity
which we all the more surely receive from
greatness of soul and mastery of mind over
matter, the stronger are the hindrances in the
surmounting of which it is manifested. After
he had become aware that his life was draw-
ing to a close, his only anxiety had been to
remain true to himself to the end, and amid
physical pain and discomfort, so far as circumstances permitted, to retain his freedom
of mind and intellectual activity, and to re-
move the sting from his suffering, by consi-
dering it in its connection with the general
order of things. With life he had ended and
cast behind him all the contests and vexa-
tions it had brought him; and in order not to
have this frame of mind disturbed, ever since
his illness had assumed a decided character
he read absolutely nothing more of all that
was written with respect to his last work.
The letters of counsel with which, from want
of judgment and importunity he was troubled,
he laid aside unread. He reflected on his
own life with the same objectivity as he had

before, as a biographer, considered that of his
heroes, and he endeavoured to make plain to
himself in the one, as he had done in the
other, why his life had fashioned itself under
the given conditions thus, and not otherwise.
Yet he did not withdraw himself from the
interest in life still possible to his condition;
he made use of every tolerable moment for
reading or for correspondence; he entered
constantly with his old lively interest into the
concerns and works of his friends; he repaid
with kindly thanks every service that could
be rendered to him; he extolled his fate in
having a son as his physician, to whom in
wearisome hours of suffering he could open
his innermost nature, while their mutual relation thus reached its consummation. After
his daughter's last visit he rejoiced in the
twin grandchildren with which she had presented him; and he addressed sweet little
poems to the little ones whom he was to see
no more, but who, as he wrote to me at the
close of the year in his last letter, hovered
round him like two genii, brightening his sick-
room. The poetic art, whose votary he had
secretly been all his life, did not refuse her

gifts to the dying man. I have been permitted to insert here a few of these poems, which will exhibit his frame of mind far better than any delineation made by another. In the first place, therefore, may stand these lines to his son :—

> Ever in the room of sickness,
>   Like a morning star thou art ;
> Suffer not such ray of brightness
>   Too long from me to depart.
>
> As to youth thou grew'st from boyhood,
>   And from youth becam'st a man,
> I shall gladly see completed
>   What with promise fair began.
>
> Though my powers have waxed feeble,
>   Though my life is nearly run,
> I have meanwhile gained possession
>   Of a friend as well as son.
>
> Only fear not ! do not tremble !
>   In the night-time stars appear,
> And beside the bitterest waters
>   Gushes forth a fountain clear.

Among the little poems suggested by the birth of his twin grandchildren the two following may be inserted :—

I.

TO MY DEAR DAUGHTER GEORGINE.

> From the far-off spot I love
>   Towards me the sweet rumour flies,
> That a blessing twain enshrined
>   In the tiny cradle lies !

Quickly into serious truth
  Higher powers have changed our jest,
And instead of one fair boy,
  Two are welcomed to thy breast.

Yes, be joyful ! let no care
  Cast its shadow 'cross the gleam !
Every morning brings its counsel,
  Every night-time has its dream.
As the trefoil of thy children
  Thou hast cherished until now,
So this two-leaved blossom will
  Underneath thy nurture grow.

And how great, how glorious !
  Even here does nature show ;
When the stem inclines to wither,
  Richer do the branches grow.
And the old man, on his death-bed,
  Feels his heart with courage rife ;
For with death's dull languor mingled
  Is the hope of fresh young life.

2.

A WISH.

Over the Neckar,
  Over the Rhine,
Once more to wander
  Were gladly mine.

The seven mountains
  Once more to see,
Where healthful breezes
  Blow soft and free.

Then to the city
  I next would roam,
Which won the treasure
  That blessed my home.

The nouse I would search for
The streets about ;
Mother and children
All lŏoking out.

And in the chamber,
The cheerful spot,
Two sweet twin babies
Lie in the cot.

Shade the eyes gently
From too much light ;
Ye alone see me
Without affright.

Sleep on calmly,
As children do ;
Soon will be sleeping
Grandfather too.

At Christmas 1873 he sent his daughter
the following lines, full of tender feeling :—

Amid feasting and light,
Amid looks of delight,
Rejoice with the gay.
Of thy father no thought
Must with sadness be fraught,
Though vigour and health have fled from him for aye.

In suffering and pain
One joy will remain,
One cup of delight :
'Tis thy children and thee,
In varying degree—
His evening is darkening : ye bless him with light.

Unlamenting may'st thou
Recall even now
The days that are past ;
Those who good have received,
Must in nowise be grieved,
That the dream should not still to eternity last.

> Though my memory is all
> My legacy small,
>   Yet I leave it thee here ;
> Undivided we stay,
> And when lonely thy day,
> Thou'lt think of thy father, and he will appear.

  , The last thing that Strauss wrote in verse are a few touching lines, which he addressed, soon after those just quoted to his daughter, on December 29, to a lady highly esteemed by him, the daughter of one of his earliest and nearest friends. He compares his failing life to an expiring light and a fading sound, and he concludes with the words :—

> Feeble still, and waning,
>   Yet bright, and pure, and wise,
> Be this expiring glimmer,
>   This echo as it dies ;

and in this he expressed his own innermost feelings. He made no demand upon nature that she should spare him aught that her course and her laws required ; all the more, however, he made the demand upon himself, that he should submit to these laws, that he should be enabled to render suffering a matter for moral and mental activity, and should even find benefit in pain. And thankfully he

testified in his letters and poems that he had
not failed in so doing, that for the most part
bright and even cheerful spirits visited him,
and that his present experiences yielded nothing that could perplex him in his kindly
optimism. Above all, the course of public
affairs proved refreshing and reviving to him.
If, as a true son of the people, he had been
filled with enthusiasm in the contest with the
Gallic foe, and had taken part in it as an
author, his joyful concurrence in the contest
with the foes of our mental freedom and independence was of course no less assured, and
he welcomed with undivided approval the
latest progress of affairs in this direction and
the writings which appeared in connection
with it. The last thing which he wrote, the
postscript to a letter of February 4, 1874,
was as follows:—'Good luck for to-mor-
row, the opening of the Diet. These are
main matters, compared with which our small
ills vanish.'

In this grand spirit he treated his sufferings, and by this treatment he alleviated
them; and if friends who visited him, parted
from him with feelings such as Plato has

depicted at the conclusion of his ' Phædo,' they were justified in entertaining them : in spite of the differences of position and character, they saw before them a philosopher of the present century, treading the last journey with the same composure and courage, the same clearness and freedom of mind, as the old philosopher in Plato. He himself even in his last few days was reading ' Phædo ' in the original.

His malady had slowly but steadily increased. On January 4 an experienced surgeon, Simon of Heidelberg, performed an operation long urged by the son, but always deferred by the patient himself, upon the tumour before mentioned. The operation itself was successfully performed without much pain, and without the application of chloroform ; but it could not check the progress of the evil. Fever set in, and the increasing weakness made it impossible for Strauss to receive visits ; besides his son and his nurse, none but an old friend, Pastor Rapp, residing in Stuttgart, in whose house and society he had formerly passed many cheerful and pleasant hours, kept up his intercourse with others, although he still continued to occupy himself mentally and could even write letters. Yet even on January 27 he spent his last birthday in the society of his son and son-in-law, tolerable, and even cheerful. On February 7, towards evening, a sudden change for the worse appeared, and the same night his nurse, who against his will was sitting up in the adjoining room, saw herself obliged to summon his son by telegraph. He arrived at four in the morning, and found his father no longer conscious. At six o'clock the sick man fell into a light slumber; towards noon he breathed his last peacefully in the arms of his son, and lay in death as calm as if asleep.

Strauss himself had left directions with regard to his funeral. He wished to be buried simply and without pomp in a pine-wood coffin; all participation of the Church in the ceremony was to be dispensed with, but on the day of the funeral a sum of money was to be given to the local authorities for the poor. On February 10, therefore, he was buried without ringing of bells or the presence of a clergyman, but in the most suitable manner, and amid the lively sympathy of all far and near.

In addition to his son and his twin grandchildren, numerous friends, especially from Stuttgart, were present; several officers also of the garrison took part in the funeral, and the Stuttgart Polytechnicians sent a deputation. The coffin was covered with fresh laurel, which was lavished on all sides, and an almost boundless procession of friends followed it. Three Stuttgart friends spoke at his grave a few hearty words of remembrance and farewell—Director v. Binder, who for more than fifty years, ever since his admission at Blaubeuren, had been united with him in unclouded friendship; Professor Reuscher, likewise one of his earlier and more intimate friends; and Dr. Ruoff, a relative of the deceased.

Throughout Germany, and far beyond her limits, a feeling of painful interest was excited by the tidings of Strauss's death, as it had been before aroused by those of his illness, amongst all who appreciated mental greatness, whether approving or not of his opinions. It was only a passing discord in this general

feeling when adherents of the Stuttgart
pietist party could not forbear performing a
scene of ugly inquisitorial malice on the fresh
grave-mound of the dead, by setting on foot
a feeling of agitation against his friend
Binder on account of the words which he
had spoken at Strauss's grave, even without
accurately knowing their purport, and in rais-
ing accusations against him in the public
papers, the falsity of which at length truth-
loving members of the party felt themselves
bound to testify.

Among the sound part of our people, far
and wide spread the feeling, a feeling expressed almost universally by the press, that in
Strauss had passed away not merely one of
their most clever and agreeable authors, and
one of their acutest thinkers, but also a scientific character of the highest rank, unwearied
in searching after truth, and fearless in expressing his convictions. What he was, however,
beyond this in all human relations of life to
all those who were more closely connected
with him, how much they have lost in him,
and how much more they have preserved as
an imperishable possession, those even to

whom this happiness has not been permitted will be enabled to form at any rate an approximate idea even by such an imperfect sketch of his life as has here been possible.

.

LONDON : PRINTED BY

SPOTTISWOODE AND CO., NEW-STREET SQUARE

AND PARLIAMENT STREET

.